A GERRY ANDERSON PRODUCTION

THUNDERBIRDS™

PERIL IN PERU

A GERRY ANDERSON PRODUCTION

THUNDERBIRDS™

PERIL IN PERU

By John Theydon
Edited by Chris Dale

Anderson Entertainment Limited
The Corner House, 2 High Street, Aylesford, Kent, ME20 7BG

Thunderbirds: Peril in Peru by John Theydon.
First published in 1966 under the title 'Calling Thunderbirds'.

Hardcover edition published by Anderson Entertainment in 2021.

www.gerryanderson.co.uk

ISBN: 9781914522185

Editorial director: Jamie Anderson
Editor: Chris Dale
Cover design: Marcus Stamps

Typeset by Rajender Singh Bisht

TABLE OF CONTENTS

CHAPTER ONE

THE EARTH SHAKES

Remote from shipping lanes and looking a mere pinhead of green and white from any supersonic planes screaming far above, the tiny tropical island which was the secret base of International Rescue lay like a jewel on the calm surface of the Pacific.

Scott Tracy, returning from a routine security check of the island, walked up the palm-flanked causeway from the lagoon and went through a wicket door into the hidden hangar in the base of the cliff below the concrete and glass house.

Gordon and Virgil, two of his four brothers, wearing light blue overalls, were busy servicing Thunderbird Two, the huge jet aircraft which could convey heavy rescue equipment to the four corners of the world at five thousand miles an hour.

"Sure does my heart good to see folk working," Scott said cheerfully. "But where's Brains?"

"He's been up in the lab all morning," Gordon said, removing his coppery head from a jet intake.

"Holding a computer conference," Virgil grinned. "He's probably got some weird and wonderful new bee in his bonnet."

"More likely he's giving 'em a pep talk," Scott chuckled. "Telling 'em how to do their job. I'll go up and see him. I've been thinking—"

"Gee!" Virgil gasped, turning to look in feigned astonishment at Gordon. "So *that* was the strange noise we heard!"

7

"Yeah. I figured it was a hurricane blowing up, but it was just big brother's brain awakening from an age-long stupor."

"Wise guys, huh?" Scott snorted good-humouredly, stepping into the small service elevator. "Remind me to punch your noses some time when I'm not so busy."

Scott entered the laboratory workshop. Brains, the young scientist and inventor whose genius had created the wonderful craft and equipment which served International Rescue so well, was bending over a bench beside a computer. His dark hair was ruffled and his cheeks were smeared with grease.

"Say, Brains—"

"Quiet, please!" Brains cut in, with a peremptory gesture of his hand.

Scott crossed the room and peered curiously at the complicated piece of equipment Brains was manipulating. Coloured lights were flashing and a needle was tracing an erratic line on a graph.

"Crockery rattles. Picture falls from wall. Few bells ring," muttered Brains.

Scott slowly turned his gaze from the instrument to Brains. Had it happened at last? Had over-stimulation of his mind sent poor old Brains round the bend?

The young scientist seemed to become aware of Scott's anxious scrutiny and blinked at him through his big horn-rims.

"Oh—er—hallo, Scott. I didn't hear you come in."

"Nevertheless you told me to shut up!"

"Did I? I'm terribly sorry, Scott. I did not intend to be rude, but I guess I was so engrossed in my new invention." He indicated the instrument. "This is my seismoclinometer."

"Your what?"

"Well, it's a device for giving warnings of impending earthquakes, Scott. As you know, we've had warning systems for hurricanes and tsunamis and volcanic eruptions for a long time now and hundreds of thousands of lives have been saved in consequence. But so far earthquakes have proved an—er—insurmountable problem."

"But *you've* surmounted it?"

"I am encouraged to hope so, Scott. An hour ago I thought I detected indications of a tremor in Japan. Just on the off chance I radioed a warning to the Japanese Geodetic Control. A few moments ago I registered a fourth degree shock."

"Fourth degree? What's that mean?"

"Not very serious, I am glad to say. A slight shaking that would be noticed by most people indoors. Crockery would rattle and pictures fall from walls and—"

"A few bells would ring? So that's what you were muttering about just now?"

"Yes, Scott. But if the shock had been a severe one, involving damage to buildings, my warning would undoubtedly have saved lives."

"That's great! You're a knock-out, Brains."

Brains blinked. "Oh, little of the credit is due to me, Scott. Seismologists have been trying for over a hundred years to get warnings of earth shocks. I've merely collated their data and fed it into a computer. Even so my system is far from perfection. Yet for thousands of years birds and animals have been known to flee from an earthquake zone before the actual shock occurred."

"You're too modest, Brains. This device of yours seems to be the cat's whiskers. Can you give me a demonstration?"

"One can't conjure up shocks to order, Scott. But we could try. The Pacific seaboard of South America, for instance." Brains turned some controls. "There are constant small tremors occurring there. First degree which can be recorded by seismographs only, or second degree shocks felt by a few people on the higher floors of a building. Indeed, it is said that in Chile and Peru the natives only begin to worry when they *don't* feel a tremor for some time…"

He broke off, suddenly tense.

"What's the matter?" Scott asked.

Brains pointed to a tube in which mercury was leaping beneath a red flashing light.

"Look, Scott! That indicates that tremendous subterranean pressure is building up off the Peruvian coast." Brains rapidly punched buttons on the computer. It hummed and ticker tape began to spill out like ribbon from a magician's hat. Brains grabbed it and began to read.

"Earth shock imminent. Epicentre south-south-east of Lima."

"Will it be a bad shock?" Scott asked anxiously.

"Degree six or seven possibly. If the epicentre is deep in the mountains perhaps it will not be serious. But there may be damage to badly constructed houses. I must radio a warning."

"How long before it hits them?"

Brains shrugged. "One cannot be sure. It may be an hour, perhaps less."

"Okay. Get that warning through, Brains. I'm going to see Dad."

Scott hurried through into the lounge where his father was dictating a report to Tin-Tin, the lovely raven-haired Eurasian girl who often served as his secretary.

Jeff Tracy looked up, a faint smile creasing his craggy face as he sensed Scott's excitement.

"What's eating you, son?"

Scott quickly explained Brains' earthquake forecast.

Jeff frowned. "I knew he was working on something like that, but results seemed incredibly remote."

"Dad!" Scott broke in urgently. "This may be a false alarm. But equally it could mean great devastation, even if they do take notice of Brains' warnings and evacuate the danger zone. They may need all the rescue workers they can get."

"And you figure International Rescue should be right there, just in case it's needed, huh? You're right, son." Jeff glanced at a chart on his desk. "You can get to Lima in twenty minutes from take-off. Get cracking! I'll launch Thunderbird Two as soon as I hear from you what equipment will be necessary to supplement local resources."

"Okay, Dad. I'm on my way."

Scott hurried across the lounge and stood in one of the semi-circles formed on the polished floor by the scalloped edge of the carpet, his back to the wall. He raised his hands and grasped bracket lamps fixed to the wall on either side of his head.

Hidden machinery whirred softly and a section of the wall at his back pivoted, taking him with it. The inner side of the wall panel slid smoothly into place and the lounge looked just as it was before, complete with an identical pair of wall lights.

Beyond the wall Scott, still grasping the lights, paused for an instant, looking down proudly at the slim length of his rocket plane Thunderbird One, which stood on its tail in a vast concrete pit hangar beneath the house. Then he removed his hands from the lamps and a moving bridgeway carried him across the gap into the nose cone of the ninety-foot vessel.

In the small equipment-packed control cabin, he pressed a button on the arm of the gimbal-slung pilot seat, and a panel slid back to reveal his uniform with the extended hand insignia of International Rescue on the blue shoulder band.

While he put on his uniform, Thunderbird One moved automatically to its launch ramp and then slid smoothly downwards out of the hangar into the launch pit beneath the swimming pool.

In the lounge above, Virgil and Gordon, still in their greasy overalls, alerted by the action stations alarm, had joined their father and Tin-Tin. Jeff briefed them on the situation.

"You two boys stand by. We should be hearing from Scott inside twenty minutes, if we don't get a prior call from the danger zone."

They watched as the swimming pool moved slowly

sideways, sliding beneath the stone-flagged patio to reveal the gloomy launching pit below.

There was nothing for them to do. Automatic controls ensured trouble-free working.

Rocket motors thundered, amplified by the confines of the pit. The red nosecone of Thunderbird One appeared, gleaming in the sun. With a whooshing roar it slowly rose on flaring rocket gases, then accelerated towards the cloudless blue of the sky.

Jeff turned and crossed the room to his desk. A flick of a switch and a brass ashtray rose like a hinged flap to expose a microphone-speaker.

"Space station from base," he said. "Come in, John."

On the wall above him, one of the portrait photos of his five sons suddenly vanished, to reveal a television screen on which was the image of John Tracy in his blue and lilac space station uniform.

"Yes, Father?"

"Scott's blasted off for Peru. Brains thinks an earth shock may be imminent. Keep in constant touch with him and monitor local radio stations. If anything happens before Scott gets there, report to me immediately."

"F.A.B., Father!"

A bleeping came from Scott's portrait and it too vanished to reveal another monitor screen showing him sitting at the controls of his craft.

"Thunderbird One to base," he announced. "Changing to horizontal flight. Setting course north-north by west."

"Okay, son," Jeff said, smiling up at him. "Carry on. But for once I'm sure hoping Brains is wrong."

Scott levelled off at two thousand five hundred feet and headed north-north by west.

Although the powerful jet could fly at higher altitudes than any military supersonic craft, it flew at a height of two thousand five hundred feet only when leaving base to avoid detection by radar stations. Only by taking such precautions had Jeff Tracy been able to keep his headquarters a secret from the world. He knew there were many unscrupulous people who coveted the secrets of International Rescue.

Fifteen minutes later Scott saw the snow-capped peaks of the Andes rearing their jagged teeth above the clouds. But the ocean below him and the coastline were hidden by the mist that continually shrouds the Peruvian coastal zone, due to the cold Antarctic currents meeting the warm equatorial waters.

He switched on his microphone. "Space station from Thunderbird One. Approaching destination. Estimated time of arrival five minutes. Ground visibility nil. Reducing speed to reconnaissance and descending to five hundred feet."

"F.A.B., Scott," John said.

Scott fired his retro-rockets and the great wings unfolded. The aircraft dipped and glided through the mist.

"Any communication from destination?" he asked.

"The authorities acknowledge Brains' warnings and have evacuated all possible danger areas. Touch down at the airport, Scott. They're keeping Runway Five clear for you, although I emphasised you did not need a runway."

"F.A.B., John."

Through the grey mist he could now see the creamy waterline and the yellow white of the coastal desert strip. Thousands of seabirds screeched and whirled above the guano islands, startled by his screaming jets.

He flashed over the ancient port of Callao and saw the tall graceful white buildings of twenty-first century Lima towering through the mist against the dark backcloth of the Andean slopes.

The blinking beacons of the airport came into sight. He overshot, marking the cleared runway, and circled in a wide radius. As he zoomed back, preparing to fire the under jets to make his vertical landing, it happened.

The black and white surface of the airfield split jaggedly across as if it were a sheet of paper slashed by an invisible knife.

A giant strato-liner on the adjoining runway teetered and then nose-dived into the gap. For an instant it hung there, its great tail pointing skywards like an accusing finger, and then the gap snapped shut again, crushing the front half of the plane like gigantic nutcrackers. The tail crashed to the tarmac and burst into flames.

Sweat started on Scott's brow as he lifted Thunderbird One and flew on.

"Another minute and I might have been down there," he muttered. "I'm sure glad that was an empty plane!"

As he flew low over the coast he saw that the sea, so calm when he had come in, was now violently agitated. He swung inland again. Here and there he saw a building that had crumpled like a house of cards, but for the most part they had withstood the shock; for the people of this country had learned by many a bitter lesson how to build in order to withstand constant tremors.

When he approached the airport again, he saw that the fire-tenders had already extinguished the blazing plane. Two other planes were canted on smashed wings, but there was no other sign of damage. The pre-stressed ferro-concrete control buildings on their solid bedrock foundations had stood firm.

Scott called the tower. "Lima Tower from Thunderbird One. Is it safe to land?"

"Thunderbird One from Tower Control." The officer's voice sounded a little shaken. "Shock was of minor duration, and has now subsided. It is safe to land."

Firing the under-jets, Scott touched down between the tower and the burned-out airliner. As he opened the hatch and dropped to the ground, a jeep chased across the airfield and screeched to a halt. A uniformed official alighted.

"Welcome, señor," she said, saluting. "We are much indebted to your so-wonderful organisation for your timely warning. It is incredible that you should learn of this thing, but undoubtedly it has saved much loss of life."

"I'm glad to hear it," Scott replied. "Just how bad is the damage, señorita?"

"In the older, the poorer quarters, it is considerable, but thanks to your warning we were able to evacuate the inhabitants."

"Casualties?"

"Many, but mainly minor injuries with which the medical services can cope." The official shrugged. "A very unpleasant experience, but fortunately not a national calamity, señor. So far there have been no deaths reported."

"So far? You mean—?"

"That we must wait for reports from outlying districts before we can be sure. And there is one building in the town on which the rescuers are still working; a small restaurant in which a wall collapsed. Patrons are buried. Until we have got them out we cannot be sure if there are any fatalities."

The official clicked her heels and smiled. "Her Excellency the Mayoress has asked me to request that you will stand by in case we have difficulty, señor. We understand that your wonderful organisation has unique equipment which can deal with almost impossible situations."

"Sure," Scott smiled, "I'll stand by. Take me to this place. Maybe I can be of some assistance. But I'd like a hand with my mobile control equipment, just in case it's needed."

"Certainly, señor!"

The official blew a whistle and airport hands hurried up. Scott's control consoles were loaded into the jeep.

"And I'd like a guard put on my craft to make sure no one takes pictures of it," Scott went on. "That is vital, señorita."

"It shall be done, my friend." The official gave an order into a microphone on the jeep and two airport police cars drove out to take up guard stations by the rocket plane.

"You see, señor," the official said with a smile as the jeep, with screaming siren, hurtled out of the airport and down the wide tree-lined avenue leading to the city, "we treat you like royalty. Today you are our saviours. We shall be forever grateful to you."

Here and there a small roadside building lay in ruins. The concrete of the road was cracked in places and a huge cornice stone from a high building had plunged deep into the earth. Palm trees had been snapped like matchsticks.

On the outskirts of the city, among the older and smaller buildings, the damage was greater. The narrow streets were blocked with rubble, and stolid-faced residents were poking about in the ruins of their homes, seeking to salvage what they could of their belongings.

"Is it not incredible what damage Nature can do in a few short moments, señor?" asked the official. "She is angry and shakes the earth and there is little we can do but flee for our lives. These people here have International Rescue to thank for the fact that they are still alive this afternoon."

"Well, I guess that's why we exist, in a way," Scott smiled. "Our main job is rescuing folk who're in danger, but maybe prevention is better than cure."

Scott knew that the credit was Brains' and his alone. But for Brains' latest incredible invention, Lima might have been mourning its dead tonight.

The jeep swung into the entrance to a public square which had been cordoned off by green-uniformed police. The screaming siren parted the crowd that had gathered there, the barrier was raised and the jeep tore round the square, in which fountains still played as they had done for centuries.

On the far side heavy rescue appliances were standing by the ruins of a cafe whose once brightly coloured awning protruded like a tattered banner from a heap of masonry and rubble.

As the jeep slammed to a halt, an injured man on a stretcher was being carried from a hole, which had been tunnelled into the ruins, towards a waiting ambulance.

An official-looking grey-haired woman in civilian clothes pushed through the crowd of rescue workers and held out a welcoming hand to Scott when he alighted from the jeep. "Ah, International Rescue! The honour is great for me to meet you, señor. But for you—"

Scott was spared further embarrassing congratulations by an excited shout from the ruins.

"*Bueno!*" exclaimed the woman who had greeted him. "The last survivor, we think, has been located. And he is still alive, señor. It is with great relief that I tell you that your so welcome services will not be needed."

"All the same, Señora Mayor," Scott said. "I'll stick around for a while, just in case we're needed elsewhere."

The Mayoress bowed. "We shall be honoured, my friend."

While the injured man was being eased from the ruins, Scott returned to the jeep and contacted his father.

"Okay, Scott," said Jeff, when he'd finished his brief report. "Stay there as long as there's half a chance we may be needed. It's great to know we've already saved more lives than we could ever have hoped to save if we'd been called in *after* the 'quake. I guess Brains ought to be given the freedom of the city."

Scott signed off and returned to the ruins to watch the final rescue operation. The victim came out on a sling, strapped to a stretcher, carefully guided by rescue workers. He was unconscious. His pale handsome features were grimed with dust, his fair hair matted with blood. Scott guessed he was a year or so older than himself.

As the man was carried past him towards the ambulance, Scott found himself thinking there was something vaguely familiar about that good-looking face.

"Who is he?" he asked the official who had met him at the airport.

The woman shrugged. "An English tourist, we believe. We shall not know for certain until we have examined his papers or he recovers consciousness, señor."

There was a pause while the injured man was gently removed from the stretcher. Then his lips moved and he muttered, half deliriously, "Penny! I must tell Penny."

As the ambulance drove off, Scott looked after it thoughtfully. Where had he seen that face before?

Then a shout announced that still one more victim had been found deep down under the ruins, and he forgot about the fair-haired young man.

But he was to remember him a few days later.

CHAPTER TWO

DISTANT MENACE

The Asian Moon, riding high above the dark jungle, filtered its wan light into the clearing, and the ancient temple crouching there flung sinister shadows across the silvered grass.

The black sinuous shape of a panther loped noiselessly from the trees, then checked suddenly, regarding the temple with suspicious red-gleaming eyes. Then, with a defiant snarl, as if sensing the evil lurking there, it turned and padded away as silently as it had come.

Somewhere in the depths of that dark sea of fetid vegetation a stricken animal screeched in pain and terror. Then the hot stillness of the jungle settled down again, a stillness alive with mysterious rustlings and sibilant whisperings. Bats flitted across the clearing and disappeared amongst the massive columns supporting the temple roof.

From the distance came a soft whirring. Gradually it grew louder as high up against the Moon a helicopter appeared like a huge nocturnal bird of prey. Slowly it descended and the unseen prowlers of the jungle night were suddenly quiet, wondering, fearful.

The helicopter touched down in the centre of the clearing some yards from the temple entrance. Its vanes ceased to rotate.

In the cabin the arch-criminal known only to his few evil associates as the Hood sat for a moment looking at the temple. A malicious smile twisted his hairless face beneath a great dome of a head as bald as an egg laid by some monstrous prehistoric reptile.

"*International Rescue!*" He spat out the words in a voice

steeped in venom. "Too often have they frustrated me. But I have powers of which they know nothing. Soon I will triumph, soon their secrets will be mine!"

He laughed harshly, then took from a locker a white Oriental priest's robe, putting it on over the well-cut suit he wore.

Descending from the helicopter, he walked slowly and ponderously, a powerful ox of a man, towards the grotesque carved portals of the temple.

The religion served by the Hood was peculiar to himself. The god he worshipped was his own evil ambition. His creed was hatred of all that was good in the world, but especially of Jeff Tracy, his five sons and other members of International Rescue.

Entering the temple he descended into a great marble-paved chamber dimly lighted by flickering torches. Weird paintings on the walls seemed to writhe in evil ecstasy and hideous idols leered as if paying homage to him. Unseen presences seemed to whisper in the shifting shadows.

The Hood stopped in the centre of the chamber and turned to face a proscenium which filled the far end from wall to wall. The bead curtains screening it glittered like fire in the light of the torches.

"International Rescue! Bah!"

Again he spat out the words and his harsh guttural voice echoed through the temple as if it had conjured up an approving chorus of fiends.

Slowly he sank down on his knees and touched his bald brow to the cold marble of the floor. Then, straightening, he spread his arms towards the bead curtains. With an eerie tinkling they parted to disclose a semi-circular dais in the centre of which stood a giant bronze figure of a man in Eastern clothing. Beyond it flames leaped and hissed. Before it, at its feet, on a slowly revolving lower dais, stood six masks with eyeless sockets, disguises worn by the Hood whenever he went into the outer world on one of his evil missions.

He rose to his feet and approached the dais, his dark eyes, set deep beneath beetling black brows, glinting wickedly as he gazed up at the immobile face of the bronze image.

"Kyrano! I have need of you again, Kyrano, my half brother! And this time I shall not fail. The goddess of luck cannot always favour your accursed employer and his sons. Is it not written in the ancient books that eventually I shall triumph?"

As he paused the sinister echoes seemed to whisper, *"Thou shalt triumph, High Priest of Evil! Thou shall triumph! It is written in the ancient books."*

The Hood smiled coldly. "And when that day comes, Kyrano, when the secrets of International Rescue are mine, when their power has made me the master of the world you, and Jeff Tracy and his brood, and that daughter Tin-Tin whom you worship shall be the first to be destroyed. Heh, heh, heh!"

His savage laughter echoed away into the dark recesses of the temple. He raised his hands towards the statue's face and his eyes flashed like malignant black jewels.

"Kyrano! Kyrano! I am calling you! Can you hear me, Kyrano? Although you may be half a world away, you cannot escape me. Kyrano! Kyrano!"

On the tropical island base of International Rescue, Virgil Tracy paced the lounge uneasily, glancing at his watch.

"Over ten minutes since Scott last came through," he said.

Jeff Tracy glanced up with a smile from the report he was reading at his desk.

"I know you're raring to blast off, son, but if Scott needs heavy rescue he'll ask for it soon enough."

"Sure, but suppose he can't? Suppose there's been another earthquake and he's in trouble?"

"Better take a sedative, Virgil," grinned fair-haired Alan, the youngest of the five brothers. "You're a bag of nerves."

Virgil glared at him, and Jeff chuckled. Since his wife had died many years ago, the former astronaut had brought his sons up to a spartan regime, toughening them in mind and body against the day when his great dream of International Rescue would come true. The thought of any of them being a bag of nerves tickled him.

"Coffee, gentlemen?"

A grey-haired figure in a yellow silk Oriental robe had quietly entered the room with a tray. His face was wrinkled with a kindly smile.

Kyrano had been Jeff's servant for more years than either cared to remember, but their relationship went far deeper than that and Jeff had come to regard Kyrano's daughter Tin-Tin, whose education he had paid for, as the daughter he himself had always wanted but had been denied.

"Tin-Tin has taken a cup to Brains," Kyrano went on, moving forward to place the tray on a low table. "He does not want to leave his new experiment—*Oh!*"

Kyrano gave a little choking gasp. His eyes closed and he swayed.

"*Kyrano!*" Jeff sprang to his feet, alarmed. "What's wrong?"

But Kyrano did not hear him. A strange rustling and jangling as of distant exotic instruments filled his ears.

"No!" he gasped. "No, never again! I-I cannot—"

"You shall, Kyrano!" The voice seemed to sound in Kyrano's brain, beating against his senses with numbing insistence. "You are powerless to resist me, Kyrano. Tell me where is the secret base of International Rescue?"

"No, no!"

"KYRANO! KYRANO!" The voice thundered in his brain. "SPEAK, KYRANO!"

A dark cloud seemed to descend on Kyrano's mind. The tray crashed to the floor and with a moan he tottered and would have fallen had not Virgil flung himself forward and caught him.

His face was the colour of old putty. They laid him on the couch and presently he stirred faintly and then opened his eyes.

"What happened, Kyrano?" Jeff asked hoarsely, helping him to sit up. "Did you have another of those dizzy spells?"

Kyrano smiled weakly. "I fear I did, Mr. Tracy. I cannot understand it. They come so suddenly."

Jeff frowned. "You're getting too many of these attacks. I sure don't like it. But the Doc says he can find nothing wrong. You're one hundred per cent fit." He looked up at his sons. "One of you boys go get him a glass of brandy."

As Gordon hurried out, Jeff asked worriedly, "Can't you remember anything that happens before you pass out, Kyrano? You say they're dizzy spells, but aren't there any other symptoms?"

Kyrano passed a thin hand across his brow. "It is as if a dark cloud descends on my mind. I think I remember hearing strange noises, like musical instruments. And there seems to be a voice."

"A voice?" Jeff exchanged anxious glances with Virgil. "What kind of a voice, Kyrano? What does it say?"

"I cannot remember. It seems to be asking me questions, questions I do not wish to answer, but I cannot remember what they are."

"Strange sounds and voices?" Jeff frowned. He knew that people suffering from mental derangement sometimes imagine they hear strange sounds and voices, but Kyrano was as sane as he or any of his sons.

There was an anxious cry behind them, and a slim dark-haired figure in a pale blue kimono dashed into the room.

"Father! Father!" she exclaimed. "Are you all right?"

He smiled at her fondly. "Just a little faint, my dear."

"And worried like the rest of us, I guess," Jeff said gruffly. "He had another dizzy attack, Tin-Tin. But this time there's something else. He remembers hearing noises and a voice before he passed out."

Gordon came hurrying back with the glass of brandy,

Brains trailing behind him. Kyrano sipped the brandy, then waved it away.

"I am all right now," he said, getting to his feet. "If you will excuse me I will go and bring more refreshments."

"You will not, father," Tin-Tin said firmly, taking his arm, her pretty face severe. "You will lie down and rest. I shall get the refreshments."

Jeff watched anxiously as they left the lounge.

"Hadn't you better get the Doc out to him, Dad?" Virgil asked.

"What's the use, son? Doc can't find anything to account for these strange spells and he'd only want to take Kyrano back to a nursing home for a long period of observation. I think Kyrano would pine right away rather than leave us. But I'm beginning to think that it's not medical care that Kyrano needs."

His sons looked at him curiously.

"Then what?" asked Virgil.

Jeff began to pace the room, as he always did when he was agitated.

"Boys, there's something mighty peculiar about these attacks Kyrano has. Every attack seems to be - well, a kind of prelude to trouble for us. Up till now I've dismissed it as just a strange coincidence, but now, in view of what Kyrano just told us, I'm not so sure."

"What did he tell you, Mr. Tracy?" Brains asked, blinking curiously behind his large horn rims.

Jeff looked hopefully at the young scientist. His white lab overalls were smudged with grease, and again a smear of oil ran like a dark scar across his lofty forehead.

"Kyrano thought he remembered hearing strange sounds and a voice asking him questions. We all heard him gasping '*No, no! I cannot!*' as though he were refusing to answer. Does that suggest anything to you, Brains?"

"As we can rule out dementia, Mr. Tracy, there is only one thing that occurs to me; some form of tele-hypnosis, perhaps."

Jeff frowned. "You mean long range hypnosis?"

"Yes. I believe some of the Asiatic races - the Tibetans, for instance - have long been adept at influencing minds over quite vast distances."

"Yes. I guess that might explain it, Brains. I don't know much about these things, but - well, there'd have to be some kind of prior contact, wouldn't there? I mean, a guy can't decide to hypnotise another fellow a thousand miles away and do it just like that. Wouldn't the subject have to be someone known to the hypnotist?"

"So I should imagine, Mr. Tracy. There are authenticated cases of long range telepathy between sympathetic subjects, twins, for instance, or mothers and children." Brains blinked. "But I suppose it would be possible to have some inanimate object that would act as a medium, as a relay station for the thoughtwave transmission, as it were."

Jeff glanced at him sharply. "You mean something on this island, even something in Kyrano's possession? Maybe you've hit it, Brains. Of course, telepathy between sympathetic persons is a long way removed from hypnosis, but I wonder—"

"What's on your mind, Dad?" asked Alan.

"I haven't got all my ideas on this sorted out yet, boys, but - remember that ginger-haired guy with the glaring eyes that Scott clashed with in the Gobi desert a short while back?"

"Sure," Gordon said. "*He* had some kind of hypnotic power."

"I'll say he did," Virgil agreed with a flat grin. "He knocked you, me and Scott out cold by just looking at us that time he broke into Lady Penelope's garage at the Creighton-Ward mansion. His eyes flashed and - wham! We just blacked out like we'd been pole-axed."

"I get you, Dad," Gordon went on eagerly. "That guy's been around quite a bit when we've met with trouble on rescue jobs. He might somehow be able to work on Kyrano from a distance."

"Yeah, but why Kyrano?" demanded Virgil. "Why not Brains, who's got all the blueprints of our secrets in his head?"

"Why not any of us who go out on rescue operations?" put in Alan.

Jeff shrugged. "Could be he's got some personal contact with Kyrano, like Brains suggested. Kyrano comes from the Far East. Maybe way back in his past there's something—"

"Say, I've got a swell idea!" Virgil broke in. He looked at Brains. "Remember that brain probe you used on Scott? You got thought pictures of things he couldn't remember happening - you dug 'em out of his subconscious. Reckon you could use it on Kyrano?"

Brains blinked thoughtfully. "You mean, try to trace those strange intrusions into Kyrano's mind back to their source? Hmm, it certainly might be possible, providing Kyrano was willing, of course."

Jeff frowned. "If this character with the glaring eyes is behind what happened to Kyrano, then it's a threat to International Rescue as a whole. We already know he's made several attempts to steal our secrets and he's prepared to stop at nothing to get them. If there was some way to find out just who he is and where he hangs out…"

He broke off, looking at Brains. "Would this contraption of yours harm Kyrano?"

"It requires little power to stimulate the brain cells, Mr. Tracy. It would be no more harmful than if you were to engage a hypnotist to probe his subconscious mind."

"I couldn't bring a hypnotist here anyway, Brains. It would be too risky. He might learn things about International Rescue." Jeff glanced at the entrance to the lounge, where Tin-Tin had appeared with another tray. "But we'll see what Tin-Tin says. I know Kyrano will do anything to help me, but she has a right to veto it if she wishes."

When Tin-Tin was told of the plan she nodded eagerly. "We must do it, Mr. Tracy. I'm sure my father will wish it. And this man with the glaring eyes, it was he whom I saw in the Sahara when Brains and I were searching for the treasure in Lake Anasta. You remember how he sent us to sleep with those eyes and then tried to torture poor Brains?"

"I remember," Virgil said grimly. "We found Brains buried up to his neck in sand in the full heat of the sun."

"He is a fiend in human guise!" Tin-Tin said vehemently. "But there was something about him, something familiar that I could not place, as if he were someone I had known a long long time ago."

"Hmm! That could be the clue," Brains said thoughtfully. "But let's go and have a talk with Kyrano."

Some minutes later Kyrano sat in Brains' laboratory workshop before a computer, above which was a television monitor screen.

The others watched silently as Brains gently placed on Kyrano's grey head a helmet-shaped contraption to which was attached a maze of wires and coils. Brains made a few adjustments, then plugged in the co-axial lead to the computer.

"Please relax completely, Kyrano," he said.

He pressed a switch and moved back to stare into Kyrano's eyes.

"Relax," he said softly. "Sleep! Sleep!"

Kyrano's eyes glazed, his eyelids drooped, and he slumped in the chair.

Tin-Tin clutched at Virgil's arm.

"Take it easy, honey," he whispered. "It's going to be all right. Brains knows what he's doing."

When Kyrano was fully unconscious, Brains turned another control and the monitor screen lit up.

A whirling kaleidoscope of colour appeared on the screen and then a picture formed, a picture of the laboratory with their own anxious faces staring at them.

"It's incredible!" Alan gasped.

"That's because you haven't seen Brains work this particular magic before," Virgil said.

Now a picture of the lounge was forming on the screen. In the foreground the tray of refreshments was just visible in Kyrano's hands as he carried it towards Jeff and his sons.

"Watch carefully," Brains said. "This must be the point where Kyrano fainted. If something or someone did probe into his mind then—"

"Look!" Tin-Tin gasped, pointing at the screen.

It had gone dark. Then gradually, as if approaching slowly through a fog, a gleam of light appeared, resolving itself into the flickering glow of burning torches. The features of hideous idols emerged from the shifting shadows.

"It looks like a temple, an eastern temple," Gordon said breathlessly.

"It checks," Jeff growled. "But there must be thousands of such temples scattered throughout Asia. Can't you get us a closer identification, Brains?"

"I am sorry, Mr. Tracy. There is nothing more I can do. I cannot guide Kyrano's subconscious thoughts. We can only watch and hope."

"No! No! I cannot!"

The anguished cry broke from Kyrano's lips and his unconscious body heaved and writhed as if being tortured.

"No! No! You are evil! Evil! I cannot!"

"Switch it off, for Pete's sake!" Jeff yelled, darting to Kyrano's side.

Brains cut the main switch and the screen went blank. With a moaning sigh, Kyrano slumped back in the chair.

Brains removed the helmet. Anxiously Jeff felt Kyrano's pulse, while Tin-Tin looked on with tears in her lovely eyes.

"I'm terribly sorry, Tin-Tin," Brains said agitatedly. "I did not think—"

"You are not to blame, Brains," she said, forcing a wan smile. "Father and I agreed to the experiment."

"His pulse seems normal, just as though he's been sleeping," Jeff said. "But we'd better get him to bed."

"There is nothing wrong with me," broke in Kyrano, opening his eyes and smiling up at them. "I feel quite all right. The experiment - is it over?"

Jeff stared at him. "You don't remember anything?"

"No, Mr. Tracy."

Jeff heaved a sigh. "Well, let's just thank goodness you're okay. But we won't try that again, Brains—"

An urgent bleeping from a radio console interrupted him.

"That's Scott!" Brains said. "Emergency signal." They hurried through to the lounge, where the eyes of Scott's portrait were flashing. Jeff flicked a switch on his desk. "Come in, Scott," he said.

The portrait vanished to reveal Scott sitting behind one of his consoles. His rugged face was grim and dirt-streaked, and blood was oozing from a gash on his forehead. "Scott!" his father exclaimed anxiously. "You're hurt!"

"It's nothing much, Dad," Scott said. "I was knocked out for a few minutes by a piece of stone. There's been another shock here, a major one. It caught the folk by surprise after they'd been alerted for the first one. Many are buried, fires have broken out. We'll need all the heavy equipment you can get out to us, the Firefly, the Mole, lifting equipment, everything you can cram into a pod. And we'll need it fast."

"Okay, son," snapped Jeff. "They'll be with you in an hour."

He turned to Virgil. "You heard that. Launch Thunderbird Two. Go with him, Gordon."

"I'll pre-select the equipment by remote control, Virgil," Brains said, dashing back to the workshop.

While Gordon hurried to the passenger chute, Virgil crossed the lounge in a few quick strides and placed his back close against the large wall picture of a rocket ship.

Immediately the picture panel rotated vertically, taking Virgil with it. Now Virgil on his back was hurtling head-first down a chute. It levelled out and Virgil stopped, the chute broke at his head and feet and rotated like a railway engine turntable, then tipped, shooting him feet-first through a tunnel leading down to the roof of the huge hangar that housed Thunderbird Two.

He shot through the hatch above the cabin and came to rest before the control bank, the end of the chute automatically folding into a pilot's seat.

"Thunderbird Two from workshop," said the intercom speaker. "Take Pod Six."

"Okay, Brains," Virgil said, pressing a switch before him.

The conveyor belt bearing the six pods moved to the left. The giant aircraft settled down on its four hydraulic stilts over the vast cylindrical equipment container which automatically locked into the main fuselage.

Virgil heard Gordon hurtle from the passenger chute behind him.

"Stand by for launching," he said.

The heavy cliff-face door of the hangar swung away, and slowly the massive craft rolled forward on the wheels of the pod to the long palm-flanked concrete causeway leading to the sea. The palms angled outwards to allow the wide wings to pass.

Well clear of the cliff, the aircraft stopped and the section of the runway on which it stood tilted upwards to form a launch ramp. Behind its tail a reinforced concrete shield rose.

Rocket gases flared and hammered against it, and with a thunderous roar Thunderbird Two blasted off and streaked skywards, Peru bound.

In the flickering light of the temple flames, the Hood's smooth features were contorted with rage as he glared up at the impassive face of Kyrano's image that towered above him.

"KYRANO! KYRANO! ANSWER ME, YOU FOOL! I

COMMAND YOU TO SPEAK. WHERE IS THE SECRET
BASE OF INTERNATIONAL RESCUE?"

His voice echoed away into the sinister shadows. There was
no answer from the statue.

The Hood's nostrils dilated, and his lips writhed back from
his strong white teeth in a vicious snarl.

"I cannot get through to him again. Something must have
happened to blot out my thought transmissions. Bah!"

Then his anger faded, and a cunning smile ousted the snarl.

"But perhaps there are other ways to learn what I wish to
know," he muttered. "That blonde English woman whom I
suspect is an agent for International Rescue, the one who is
called Lady Penelope. She must know where their base is. It
should be easy to make a frail creature like that talk."

With an evil chuckle he plucked from the revolving dais
a mask with dark hair and a close-clipped moustache, then
turned and strode from the temple.

CHAPTER THREE

LADY PENELOPE ENTERTAINS

Lady Penelope languidly waved her jewelled cigarette holder at the last of the portraits in the long oak-panelled gallery of the Creighton-Ward mansion.

"And that, ladies and gentlemen," she drawled, "is the thirteenth Lord Creighton, popularly known as Curly Creighton. With him, I regret to say, that branch of the family became extinct in the nineteen-sixties."

The sightseers on the conducted tour looked suitably impressed. Then Parker, the former cracksman who was now Lady Penelope's butler, came in sight along the gallery. He caught Lady Penelope signalling to him. He moved away majestically along the gallery to join her Ladyship.

"Yes, m'lady?"

She suppressed a yawn. "Please take over, Parker, or I shall expire on the spot from sheer boredom. That would be most discourteous to our guests, don't you think, after they have all paid their entrance fees? Steer them to the exit as politely and speedily as you can, and then bring me some tea."

"Yes, m'lady."

As Lady Penelope inclined her fair head to her visitors and left with a gracious smile, Parker turned and swept regally past them.

"Now come along, you lot," he said.

Lady Penelope winced.

"Really Parker," she murmured. "You'll be losing us all our customers, and with rates and taxes as they are…"

33

She descended a private stairway to the drawing room, while Parker ushered his charges back along the gallery and down the massive staircase leading to the hall.

He failed to notice the powerful dark-haired man with a close-clipped moustache who detached himself from the rear of the procession and faded discreetly into the shadows of an alcove.

The Hood chuckled softly as he listened to Parker's voice echoing hollowly from the hall below.

"Fool!" he muttered. "He will not trouble to count the number of visitors he shows out."

Fifteen minutes later Parker, bearing a silver tray, knocked discreetly on the door of the drawing room and entered. Lady Penelope, looking round from her seat beside the great hearth, smiled warmly at him.

"Well done, Parker! Our guests left perfectly satisfied, I hope?"

"Yes, m'lady. I supplied them orl with bloodstained chips from the block on which the first Lord Creighton lost his bonce - er - I mean 'is nut in the Tower of London."

"Really, Parker! You are quite incorrigible." Lady Penelope patted a yawn. "I think we both need a little holiday, Parker, to get away from this stately home routine. A little adventure perhaps. It seems a long time since we indulged in any real excitement."

She glanced at the tea tray he had placed on the low table beside her. "What is that envelope, Parker?"

"A cable, m'lady. As I was showin' out the visitors the boy delivered it."

"Indeed?" Lady Penelope frowned as she took the envelope. "Now, who would be sending me a cable? Most of my friends would use the televisor service and Mr. Tracy would radio direct."

She tore it open and read the short cable aloud.

"HOTEL MIRANDA. LIMA.

PENNY. ON VERGE OF GREAT DISCOVERY. NEED HELP. CAN YOU JOIN ME? IF LUCK HOLDS CAN MEND FAMILY FORTUNES. LOVE GUS."

She smiled. "How intriguing! And how like Gus, eh, Parker?"

"Gus, m'lady?"

"Ah, I forgot. Of course, you have not met my cousin Gus. One of our - er - black sheep. His full name is the Honourable Augustus Montmorency Montacute Algernon Creighton-Ward. But everyone just calls him Gus to save time."

"I don't blame 'em, m'lady," Parker said, pouring tea.

"Gus is a rolling stone, Parker. So far he has gathered very little moss, I regret to say. I wonder what he's doing in Peru?"

She sipped her tea and re-read the cable. "If *luck holds can mend family fortunes*. Hmm, what does that sound like to you, Parker?"

"Well, m'lady, in view of the fact that you said the 'onourable Gus was a black sheep, I'd say 'e was goin' to crack a crib."

She raised her delicately pencilled eyebrows. "Really, Parker! I think he must have scented a treasure trove." She drained her cup and set it down gently. "Parker, about that little holiday. I think we deserve one, don't you?"

He stared at her, his craggy face registering sudden consternation. "M'lady, you wasn't thinking—?"

"Of Peru, Parker?" She smiled sweetly. "I'm afraid I was. I must confess the thought of discovering an Inca hoard intrigues me."

"You're more likely to find 'ordes of snakes an' skeeters, m'lady. And what about them earthquakes? They 'ad one only a few hours ago. Saw pictures of it on the telly. 'Orrible!"

She regarded him whimsically. "Parker, you disappoint me. Are you hinting that you don't wish to accompany me?"

"I ain't so young as I was."

"Nonsense, Parker! You look younger every day. Besides, who would drive the Rolls?"

"The Rolls? You mean you would take it, m'lady?"

"My dear Parker, I'd feel quite naked without it. But before we get too excited I think I had better check with Mr. Tracy and ascertain whether he can spare me for a while."

Parker licked his lips as he watched her turn the knob on the teapot lid. A bleeping sounded from the small speaker inside the teapot, then a moment later they heard Jeff Tracy's voice. "Lady Penelope from base. Come in, Penny. You got trouble?"

"No, Jeff. Just a yen for the wide open spaces. Can you dispense with my services for a week or so? I'd like to take a little holiday."

"Why sure. If anything breaks you can get back fast enough. Where are you going?"

She told him about the cable and he whistled.

"Say, that's a mighty strange coincidence. Thunderbirds One and Two are in Lima right now, helping with rescue operations. You've heard about the earthquake, of course?"

"Yes." Lady Penelope glanced at the cable. "The time stamp shows my cousin sent this before the earthquake. It must have been delayed."

"Well, I sure hope he's okay, Penny. Maybe going out there will be the quickest way to find out, but don't stick your pretty neck out too far. Things are mighty chaotic, Scott says. If you should need help and Scott's still out there, you'd better contact him."

"I certainly will. I'll keep in touch with you, anyway. Cheerio!"

Lady Penelope closed the teapot lid and smiled at Parker. "We'll leave as soon as I've decided on a suitable wardrobe for the trip. You'd better check the Rolls."

"Yes, m'lady."

Resigned now to his fate, whatever that might prove to be, Parker turned and left the room.

As he crossed the hall a dark-haired figure in brown stepped from behind a suit of armour.

He checked in surprise. "'Ere, wot you doin', mister?" he demanded. "Why didn't you leave with the rest—"

The word froze on his lips. He stared at the deep-set dark eyes of the other man. They were flashing balefully. Rays of light seemed to stab into his eyes like white-hot needles. He wanted to raise his hands to shield them, but his body seemed to be drained of strength. He tried to cry out, but no sound came from his tightening throat.

Then his legs buckled under him and he went down, darkness swirling around him.

Behind his mask, the Hood's teeth bared in a contemptuous grin.

"Poor weak fool! Against my powers he is as helpless as a child. Now for the woman."

He stepped over Parker's unconscious form and made for the door of the drawing room.

Lady Penelope, her well-manicured hands clasped about one nylon-clad knee, gazed reflectively at the ornate plaster ceiling.

"It is a little difficult," she mused. "In the coastal desert one is likely to be fried, I understand, and in the Andes one could be frozen. And then of course there might be social occasions in Lima for which one would need to be prepared. It seems I shall need quite a wardrobe."

She tensed. The faintest clicking sounds had come from behind her, but her hearing, made animal acute by countless brushes with danger, detected it like a sensitive microphone.

Without altering her pose, she turned her blue eyes to gaze at the glittering chandelier in the centre of the ceiling. A dozen miniature mirrors reflected the pigmy image of a dark-haired man in a brown suit.

She sighed and picked up one of the cigarette holders on the table.

"It would have been more polite to have knocked," she drawled, languidly turning her head to smile at the intruder, "but do come in."

Where had they met before? The face of the man with its very close-clipped moustache was unfamiliar, yet there was something about him - those dark, cunning eyes, perhaps?

He came towards her, moving in spite of his powerful build noiselessly with cat-footed lightness on the deep pile of the carpet. Like a beast of prey, Lady Penelope found herself thinking.

"I don't usually receive visitors at this hour," she went on. "But since you are here, I'll order fresh tea."

She reached out towards the tasselled bell-rope beside the fireplace.

"Don't touch it," the Hood rasped, taking a gun from his pocket. "Though your stupid fool of a butler would not answer if you did ring."

Lady Penelope's smile broadened and dimples appeared in her satin smooth cheeks.

"Dear me, you must be one of those dreadful gangsters one reads about!"

With one careless hand she brushed a straggling lock of her honey-coloured hair from her brow, with the other put the cigarette holder between her rose-petal lips. "You don't mind if I smoke, Mister - er?"

"Hood!"

He chuckled evilly as he came closer with that silent menacing tread, the gun held steady in his powerful hand.

His voice was harsh and guttural, "You may smoke, Lady Penelope. Perhaps it will help you to think. I have some questions to ask you, and I am most anxious to get the right answers." He bared his teeth in a cold smile. "It will be too bad for you if I don't."

"Really, Mister Hood! I think I must warn you that I'm absolutely hopeless at these quiz games. A very poor student, you know. At one time it was seriously feared I might become a juvenile delinquent."

"Silence! You talk too much, my lady. If you were the fool

you are trying to pretend to be you would not be employed by International Rescue."

As he spat out the name his dark eyes gleamed with hate.

"International Rescue?" she echoed, eyes widening in wonder. "Of course, I have heard of them, Mister Hood. Who hasn't? But employed by them? Why, my dear sir. I couldn't even rescue poor pussy from the well!"

"Where is their base?" he grated. His eyes flashed fire as he leaned forward threateningly. "You will tell me or—"

He broke off with a gasp as a tiny missile sped from the empty cigarette holder in Lady Penelope's mouth like a dart from a blow pipe and burst between his eyes, to eject a pungent cloud of gas.

As he staggered back, his free hand pawing at his smarting eyes, he had a bleared glimpse of Lady Penelope launching herself out of her chair towards him.

He tried to line his gun on her, but she seized his wrist in fingers that had suddenly become bands of steel. A heave and a jerk and with a startled yell he came off his feet and hurtled across the room to land on his neck. His gun skittered away out of reach.

Half-blinded by gas and rage, he scrambled to his feet and charged furiously at the blurred slim figure which advanced deliberately towards him. She sank on one knee and he felt his foot seized.

The next thing he knew he was hurtling backwards like a diver from a springboard. There was a tinkling crash as he hit a leaded window and then a flower bed seemed to come rushing up to meet him.

Lady Penelope gazed down sadly from the broken window as he staggered to his feet.

"Dear me!" she murmured. "The gardeners *will* be annoyed. The chrysanthemums promised to be so good this year."

Choking with rage, the Hood shook his fist at her then dashed away into the shrubbery.

"What a horrible man," she mused. "He was positively cross with me." She withdrew her head and frowned at the damaged window. "I shall have to get Parker to board it up before we leave. But first, perhaps I'd better go and see what has happened to the poor fellow."

She left the drawing room to find Parker sitting on the hall floor, dazedly rubbing his face.

"Them eyes," he muttered. "Them 'orrible eyes! I've seen 'em somewhere before."

"I'm sure you have, Parker," she said, helping him to his feet. "I think he must be the man who stole that - er - thing from outer space. We've had trouble with him recently. If you remember he struck you and the Tracy boys unconscious in the garage with the power of his eyes."

She frowned. "I'm afraid I got a little rough and tossed him through the window. Perhaps I should have detained him. I'm sure Mr. Tracy would have liked a word with him."

"I'd like to 'ave a word with 'im meself," Parker growled, flexing his powerful fingers and scowling. "I'd wring 'is blinkin' neck so far round he'd see where he was comin' from."

"Before we leave I think I'll warn Mr. Tracy about him."

When she had dressed and packed for the journey, she called International Rescue and told Jeff Tracy about the man with the glaring eyes who had called himself Hood.

"Hood?" Jeff repeated. "Doesn't ring a bell, but I guess he wouldn't give you his real name. It's kind of curious he should call on you, Penny."

"Why?"

"Only this morning we were talking about that guy. It's my hunch he's the cause of those dizzy spells Kyrano gets now and then. Brains figures someone's trying to get information about International Rescue from Kyrano by tele-hypnosis. Seems he's now switched his attention to you."

"Oh, I *do* wish I hadn't got quite so rough with him, at least not without capturing him first. Maybe I'd have been able to - er - *persuade* him to talk about himself."

"I doubt it, Penny. His kind don't squeal. But they don't give up easily, either, so keep those blue eyes peeled for trouble."

She laughed. "I don't have to. If it's there, I smell it."

"Sure, I can believe that."

As she signed off, Parker came in, wearing his chauffeur's livery. He stared at the small mountain of luggage.

"Cor! I thought we was goin' for a week or two, m'lady, not a couple of years."

"Don't be silly, Parker. To a girl a constant change of attire is a tonic as good as a—"

"Cuppa?"

"Precisely, Parker. Which reminds me, don't forget the tea set and several packets of my favourite brand. I don't know what they drink in Peru."

"Dragon's blood, it wouldn't surprise me," he said gloomily, picking up some of the luggage and walking out to the car.

The big six-wheeled pink Rolls-Royce was standing on the drive outside the white columned portico.

"I hope you haven't forgotten your own luggage," Lady Penelope said, as she settled into the luxurious back seat.

"Don't worry, m'lady," he said, getting into the driving seat and pressing the control button that closed the gull-wing transparent canopy. "I've prepared meself against every h'eventuality from h'equatorial 'eat to frost bite. Also, I've got several bottles of quinine and snake-bite serum. Where to, m'lady?"

"Smugglers Cove."

"You mean we're going to use the yacht?"

"Why not? This is supposed to be a holiday…but do keep a sharp eye on the monitor screen, Parker. I have a feeling we may be followed."

"By that bloke with the 'orrible eyes?"

"Yes, Parker."

But by the time they reached the narrow entrance to the

deserted little cove on the south coast which Lady Penelope owned, there had been no sign of pursuit.

"Looks like you scared 'im off, m'lady."

"I wonder?" she mused. The car came to a standstill on the strip of sand between the towering limestone cliff and the placid blue water. "In a way I hope not - just in case Cousin Gussie's scheme should turn out to be another flop. It would help to liven things up."

Parker sighed as he put the end of Lady Penelope's cigarette holder in a tiny hole in the cliff. A massive section of the cliff face swung up from water level to reveal the sleek blue and white lines of a powerful ultra modern ocean-going motor yacht, on whose bows was the name *Seabird IV*.

There had been three predecessors, but all had been sunk in line of duty during Lady Penelope's bitter battles with ruthless international crooks.

Slowly and gracefully the yacht slid from its secret cave-berth into the bay. When it was clear, the cliff-face door automatically closed behind it, leaving nothing to betray the presence of the berth.

"Drive on, Parker," Lady Penelope ordered, when he returned to the driving seat.

"Yes, m'lady."

Parker drove down the beach into the water. He touched a button on the dashboard and the car's hydrofoils took its great weight, buoying it up, and the vortex aquajet powerpack on the rear hydrofoil drove it across the bay towards the yacht.

As the Rolls got within range, an invisible ray caused a hatch to rise at water level and Parker steered the car into the bomb-proof hold beyond.

The hatch closed again, powerful machinery whined, and the water was pumped out of the hold.

Parker opened the air-tight canopy and helped Lady Penelope out of the rear seat.

She led the way towards the door which had slid open at

the stern of the hold. "Let us adjourn to the cabin lounge and have a nice strong cup of tea to fortify us against the terrors of the deep blue sea."

"By the way, m'lady," Parker said presently, as the yacht sped out of the cove and Lady Penelope turned the controls over to the auto-pilot, "just 'ow far is it to Peru?"

"Oh, roughly seven thousand miles."

Parker nearly dropped his cup of tea. "Seven thousand?" he gulped.

"Bear up, Parker! The weather charts are set fair, and we shan't go all the way by sea. I think we'll make for Panama and then take the Rolls over the Pan-American Highway."

"Thank Pete for that," sighed Parker, "And I 'ope them weather charts is right."

Far above the speeding streamlined yacht the Hood's helicopter hovered. He regarded the blip on his radar screen with great satisfaction.

"Our lady friend has some remarkable toys," he muttered. "Like the car, the boat shall be mine when I have learned what I wish to learn and have disposed of her. Meanwhile..."

He switched on an auto-tracker, retracted the 'copter vanes, and like a black bullet the powerful craft hurtled across the grey waste of the Atlantic on the trail of *Seabird IV*.

CHAPTER FOUR

THE LADY VANISHES

"To think," Lady Penelope said dreamily, gazing about her at the white-capped mountain peaks which towered against the clear sky, "that the Conquistadores may have come this way."

"You don't say, m'lady?" Parker replied politely, his eyes fixed on the broad white highway that wound into the misty distance before the gleaming bonnet of the speeding Rolls. "I'm afraid I haven't been in the Creighton-Ward service long enough to 'ave had the honour of meeting the family."

"Too true, Parker," she laughed. "They were the Spanish conquerors of Peru. I think one of my remote ancestors had the pleasure of meeting some of them. He was with Sir Francis Drake or Frobisher, or would it have been earlier than that?"

"Lumme! That's goin' back a bit, m'lady."

"Yes. Legend says that our family fortune began with the spoils my ancestor captured from a Spanish galleon returning from Peru. So you see history repeats itself, Parker!"

"You mean now the 'onourable Gus is looking for more loot - er - I mean treasure in Peru?"

"Yes, Parker."

They had left Panama that morning, after a few discreet strings pulled by Lady Penelope had enabled her to leave *Seabird IV* in the safe custody of the world naval base.

Now they were high up in the Cordilleras of Colombia and already the Ecuador border was less than fifty miles away.

A twelve-wheeled goliath of a truck loomed up ahead. The

Rolls screamed past it, leaving the swarthy-faced driver with his eyes popping in wonder.

"*Sacramento!* Never have I seen a car like that. It flies without wings."

An hour later they were bypassing Quito.

"The highest capital in the world, Parker," she said. "On our way back perhaps we'll drop in and have a look at the cathedral."

"Lumme," thought Parker, "she talks about coming back before we get there and there's all them snakes and earthquakes and things yet."

Where the highway dipped into a wooded valley, Lady Penelope said, "We're just about halfway, Parker. I think this would be an appropriate place to stop for afternoon tea, don't you?"

"Very well, m'lady."

Parker pulled off the road into a gravelled lay-by among the trees. While Lady Penelope smoked and stretched her legs, Parker got water from a mountain stream and put the kettle on the paratrooper stove.

"Who would think we were almost on the equator, Parker? The climate is most agreeable."

"Yes, m'lady. But I 'ope that goes for the local population, too. Wot was that thing I saw slinking through the bushes over there, sort of reddish yellow?"

"A puma, I expect, Parker. Quite harmless unless it's attacked or starving, which would hardly be the case here. Do relax! We're as safe here as we were on the Creighton-Ward estate—"

The words died on her lips as the ground seemed to heave under her feet, and the kettle toppled from the stove and crashed to the ground, shooting its near-boiling water over Parker's feet.

His mouth went dry as he stared at the ground. It seemed to be rippling like a stream in a stiff breeze.

Then suddenly everything was still again, deathly still.

"W-wot was *that*, m'lady?" he asked hoarsely.

She drew on her cigarette. "Oh, just a minor earth tremor, Parker. Nothing to worry about."

He raised his eyes resignedly to the skies where the dark shape of a condor wheeled majestically against the blue.

"Nothing to worry about, she says. We're as safe 'ere as if we was in the old h'ancestral 'ome."

With a sigh he refilled the kettle and made tea. Then opened a portable table and laid a lace cloth on it.

"Two lumps, Parker?" Lady Penelope drawled, taking her seat.

"Yes, m'lady!"

As they drank a bleeping came from the teapot. Lady Penelope turned the knob and lifted the lid.

"International Rescue calling Lady Penelope," said Jeff Tracy's voice. "Can you read me, Penny?"

"Loud and clear, Jeff. We ought to, we seem to be almost as high as the space station."

"How are you making out?"

"Fine. We expect to reach Lima in three or four hours. Are the boys still there?"

"Sure. They're doing a great job. The Firefly put out some fires that were getting out of hand. Now the boys are helping to rescue buried folk with the Mole. Guess they'll still be there when you arrive, Penny. But I reckon you're going to have trouble finding accommodation."

"I'm used to roughing it, Jeff. Perhaps Parker and I can find some way to help?"

"I'm sure you will. By the way, any sign of that fellow, Hood?"

"No. We've had a very uneventful journey so far."

"Good. But don't be certain you've given him the slip. He trailed Scott to the Gobi a while back, so Peru shouldn't present any problems to a determined guy like that. So long. Keep in touch, Penny."

As she closed the teapot lid, a soft whirring sounded above. She looked up. A black helicopter was skimming over the valley.

"That's strange, m'lady," Parker said. "I've never seen a 'copter like that before, and it ain't got no registration markings."

"You're right, Parker." Lady Penelope thoughtfully watched the strange helicopter zooming up towards the rocky rim of the valley. "I wonder if I was correct when I told Jeff Tracy that there was no sign of the mysterious Mr. Hood?" She got to her feet. "I think we'll press on, Parker."

Parker gathered up the tea things. "D'you think it would be advisable to keep the front cannons h'elevated as a precaution, m'lady?"

"It would do no harm, Parker. But I don't feel we have much to fear from the gentleman yet. When we had that little – er - difference of opinion in the drawing room, he was most anxious to get certain information from me. While there is a chance of getting it I don't think he will be very rough. But if he does try anything—"

"Yes, m'lady?"

She smiled sweetly as she got into the Rolls.

"This country is most suitable for retaliatory action. We can take what measures we think fit without having to worry about causing a scene, can't we? Carry on, Parker! Beyond Cuenca we'll drop down to the coastal highway and get a breath of sea air."

"Yes, m'lady."

Parker swivelled the six wheels and drove the car sideways onto the highway, then triggered the engine and sent the Rolls hurtling out of the valley.

Smoke and dust drifted over Lima like a tenuous fog, writhing between the ruins.

In the main plaza, where Scott Tracy sat at his mobile control consoles, the city looked as if it had been bombed.

Gangs were at work, as they had been for over twenty-four hours, clearing the streets and propping up buildings which were still standing but leaning at alarming angles.

Everywhere were heaps of debris with broken rafters and beams sticking up like stiffened limbs, yawning holes which had once been windows, and paving stones flung about like cards from a scattered pack.

But most of the tall modern ferro-concrete buildings, skilfully constructed to the principles of earthquake-proof architecture, still stood defiantly in spite of broken windows and cracks in their facings. It was the brick and stone buildings that had suffered most.

Now that the short tropical twilight had come, a few electric lights were showing, sickly yellow lamps fed by temporary power units. Elsewhere kerosene flares burned, setting grotesque shadows leaping.

The intercom speaker bleeped and a red light flashed. Scott pressed a button and said, "Mobile control to Firefly. Come in, Gordon."

Gordon's image, seated at the controls of the fire-fighting unit, appeared on the monitor screen.

"Mobile control from Firefly. Fire extinguished. Reporting for further instructions."

Scott glanced inquiringly at the police officer who was sitting before her own mobile control console in a truck, co-ordinating the city's rescue services.

"Anywhere else you need our help, captain?"

"Thank you, Señor Tracy, but no. All fires are now under control, and there are no more reports of buried people."

"Okay," Scott smiled at Gordon. "Return to base, pal!"

"F.A.B.!"

As Gordon vanished from the screen, Virgil came through.

"Mobile control from Mole. Mission accomplished, Scott. Victims safely extracted from cellar and on way to hospital."

"F.A.B., Virgil. Report back here."

The police officer smiled approvingly at Scott as he switched off. "It is a wonderful organisation you have, señor. It works - how you say - like the clockwork, si?"

"We've spent a long time practising to deal with all sorts of emergencies, captain. It sure makes everything worthwhile when we know we're being of real help like this."

A mobile canteen drove up and the captain bought Scott a cup of coffee.

"Thanks," he said, taking it. "What's the general situation now?"

"The worst is over, señor. Now it is just a matter of clearing up, of getting things working again. That, of course, will take many days."

"Any chance of another shock?"

The officer shrugged. "That is always possible. Nature, she is unpredictable. Sometimes there are small aftershocks for days, even weeks. But you get the instinct about these things when you have lived with them all your life, you understand. I do not think there will be anything very serious now. A minor tremor now and then, perhaps."

"Sure glad to hear it," Scott said, sipping his coffee. "Things look bad enough as it is."

"They could have been much worse, señor. If the epicentre of the 'quake had been right under the city the damage would have been colossal. But it seems to have been in the mountains to the south, towards Cuzco."

"Cuzco? That's the ancient capital of the Incas, isn't it?"

"Si, señor. *Caramba!* They knew how to build, those Incas. For seven hundred years some of their buildings have stood. Earthquakes cannot shake them."

Through the drifting smoke the Firefly appeared and came

to a halt beside the jeep. Gordon removed the helmet of his asbestos-fibre suit and cuffed sweat from his face.

"I could use some of that coffee," he grinned. "Phew! I'll have to get Brains to invent a built-in soda fountain for these suits."

As Scott got coffee from the canteen and handed it to his brother, the Mole arrived. Its conical screw boring head looked like the snout of some weird bug from an alien world nosing from the shadows.

Virgil slid back the hatch and stepped out.

"Guess that's the lot for now, boys," Scott said. "I'll report to Dad and then we'll get back to the Thunderbirds." He returned to the control consoles and got through to the tropical island base.

Jeff Tracy's craggy features appeared on the monitor screen. He nodded approval when Scott reported concisely to him.

"Good work. Swell to know you were of service. By the way, have you seen Lady Penelope yet?"

"No, father."

"She said she'd contact you when she got to Lima. She should have been there an hour ago. I can't get through to her. I'm worried, son. I'm sure that guy with the glaring eyes was trailing her. She could be in trouble, Scott. See what you can ferret out."

"Okay, Dad. Maybe the police can help. But everything's a shambles here and finding anyone who's missing will be like looking for one pebble in a landslide, I guess."

As he signed off, Virgil said, "What's happening over there?"

Scott looked round. On the edge of the square curious onlookers had gathered to stare at the International Rescue vehicles, but were being kept back by a police barrier.

A burly man in uniform was struggling in the grip of two officers.

"Take your flamin' mitts off me!" he shouted in English. "I got to see them blokes from h'International Rescue!"

"Well, I'll be!" Scott exclaimed, "that sounds like Parker."

He hurried to the barrier. Parker, hatless and dishevelled, his chauffeur's uniform grimy, stopped struggling and looked appealingly at Scott.

"Thank Pete," he gasped. "'Ere, tell these coppers I'm a pal of yours, Mister Scott."

Scott vouched for Parker and took him back to his brothers.

"Dad was just getting anxious about you and Lady Penelope," Scott said. "Where is she?"

"That's what I'd like to know, sir," Parker said, agitated. "We was on our way to the 'orspital when suddenly these blokes sprung on us and I got a cosh on the 'ead. When I woke up 'er Ladyship wasn't there."

"You mean she's been kidnapped?" Virgil asked.

"Wot else? I remembered you was here so I came to find you. If those blokes—"

"Take it easy, Parker," Scott said. "Suppose you start at the beginning? Just why were you on your way to the hospital?"

"To find the 'onourable Gus, 'er Ladyship's cranky - I beg your pardon, sir - 'er h'eccentric cousin wot's looking for treasure."

"Dad told us about that," Scott said, smiling in spite of his concern for Lady Penelope. "But why were you looking in the hospital for him?"

"Well, we went to this hotel Miranda where he sent the cable from and the manager bloke said they hadn't seen the 'onourable Gus since before the earthquake. He suggested he might have been 'urt and we ought to try the 'orspital."

"And then you got coshed? You weren't using the Rolls?"

"No, we left it outside the city, the streets being like they were."

"Did you get a good look at those fellows who jumped you, Parker? Was one of them that guy with the glaring eyes?"

"Dunno, Mister Scott." Parker scowled. "But 'e could have been behind it. We thought 'e was followin' us. Y'see, back in England 'e got into the 'ouse and threatened 'er Ladyship. Tried to make her tell him things about International Rescue. She showed 'im where to get orf. Chucked 'im out of the window."

"Gee, I sure wish I could have seen that." Gordon said.

"She'd have shown them blokes a few parlour tricks too," Parker growled, "but she never got the chance."

Scott looked at the police officer, who had been listening intently.

"You heard that, captain?"

"Si, señor. If you will give me a description of the señorita, I will alert headquarters. They will do what they can, but you will appreciate that we have our hands full and to find her in the city under these conditions…"

She shrugged, made a note of the description Scott gave her, then returned to her radio console to send the message.

Scott turned to his brothers. "She's right. There won't be much they can do. Stand by. I'm going back with Parker to investigate. Maybe there's some clue."

"Okay, Scott," said Virgil. "I'll radio Dad and tell him what's happened. If you need us, you can call us on your walkie-talkie."

As they hurried through the rubble-littered streets Scott questioned Parker again about the attack on him and Lady Penelope.

"I'm sorry, Mister Scott," Parker said gloomily. "I can't tell you no more. One of 'em had a big hat, a sombrero like blokes wear in these foreign parts, but that ain't nothin' to go on. Swipe me! I'll never forgive myself if anything's happened to 'er Ladyship. If that bloke with the 'orrible eyes 'as got her, maybe he'll torture 'er."

Scott said nothing, but a little chill rode his spine. Since International Rescue had been in operation he'd had plenty of proof that their mysterious enemy would stop at nothing to learn their secrets. There was little Lady Penelope could tell the Hood except the location of the secret island base. He could not imagine her giving that information easily, but there was a limit to what even a tough woman could stand.

"It'll be like looking for a bloomin' needle in a 'aystack," Parker growled. "Unless..."

"Unless what?" Scott asked, as he broke off uncertainly.

"That hotel manager. There was somethin' fishy about that bloke, Mister Scott. Seemed to know more than he was prepared to let on. I wonder if it was a coincidence we was ambushed just after we left the hotel?"

"Let's go and have a talk with the guy, anyway." Scott said grimly. "It's somewhere to launch off from."

The Hotel Miranda stood back from a wide avenue at the rear of a small plaza lined with lemon trees, some of which had been snapped in two. A crack zig-zagged across the square and in places paving stones had been forced up.

The hotel was one of the older buildings, two centuries old perhaps, and cracks in its white-washed walls and a huge section of cornice that had crashed from the roof showed that it had been badly shaken.

As they mounted the wide steps to the shattered glass doors a swarthy doorman in a much-braided uniform barred their way.

"Pardon, señors, but there is no accommodation. The hotel is not safe."

"We're not staying, amigo," Scott said, brushing past him and entering the foyer.

Light gleamed faintly from a massive chandelier in the centre of an ornate ceiling, from which huge patches of plaster had fallen. In the light of an oil lamp on the carved oak reception desk, a bulky man with sleek black hair and heavy-jowled face was sorting out documents and putting them into a small suitcase.

"That's the bloke," Parker muttered.

Scott crossed the plaster-littered mosaic floor, instinctively stepping over a narrow crack that had opened in it. Maybe it was just his fancy but the floor seemed to sway ever so lightly under his feet.

The manager looked up, his dark eyes lighting up with sudden interest at the sight of Scott's uniform with the extended hand insignia on the blue shoulder belt. Then the manager's glance slid past him to Parker, and Scott was sure those eyes narrowed warily.

But an instant later the manager was smiling in friendly fashion.

"International Rescue? Lima is in your debt, señor," he said in perfect English. "Is there anything I can do?"

"A little while back a young lady came in here asking for information about a guest," Scott said.

"Ah, yes. Señor Creighton-Ward." The manager shrugged. "I tell the young lady that he has not been seen since the earthquake. Maybe he has been hurt. I tell her to go to the hospital."

"Sure, but she didn't get there. Soon after she left she was attacked and kidnapped."

The man's eyebrows went up. "*Caramba!* That is unbelievable."

"Is it?" asked Scott flatly. He studied the man's suave face intently. Was he putting on an act or registering genuine astonishment? "You wouldn't know anything about that?"

"I? Señor, do you suggest that..."

The manager's voice trailed away, and the colour drained from his fleshy face. The floor beneath them was trembling. Deep down in the bowels of the earth there was a rumbling like distant thunder.

It was not the first tremor Scott had experienced, but he felt a queasy feeling in the pit of his stomach.

A solid marble pillar beyond the manager seemed to be rippling. A crack appeared in it.

"Lumme!" he heard Parker gasp behind him. "Look!"

Scott turned. Parker was pointing at the huge chandelier. It was swinging like a pendulum.

Scott watched, fascinated in spite of himself. Wider and wider swung the pendulum until it was almost touching the ceiling. Then another violent shock sent him lurching against the desk.

"Run, señors!" gasped the manager. "Run for your lives!"

He turned and darted into the office behind him.

Scott felt Parker grab his arm.

"Let's get out of here, guv!"

Sudden fear lent wings to Scott. He dashed after Parker towards the doorway. The chandelier struck the ceiling, bringing down a shower of plaster, then crashed almost at Scott's heels. A flying splinter of glass grazed his neck.

He saw Parker hurtle through one of the now-paneless doors and took a running dive after him. He hit the steps outside on his shoulder with a force that jarred every bone in his body, and rolled to the bottom. On the footway he tried to scramble to his feet, but a paving stone heaved up under him, flinging him into the roadway like a stone from a catapult.

Dazedly he was aware of Parker dragging him to his feet, and together they flung themselves across the far pavement and into a shrubbery.

Then with a thunderous roar the hotel collapsed.

CHAPTER FIVE

PARKER CRACKS A CRIB

Scott and Parker lay face down among the shrubs, hugging the earth and protecting their heads with their arms against the flying debris.

All at once there was silence and the ground beneath them was still.

Slowly they raised their heads and an icy hand seemed to close about Scott's heart when he saw through the settling dust the ruin that had once been a hotel. Another minute or so and he and Parker would have been buried underneath it.

He remembered something.

"Parker," he said, his throat hoarse from the drifting dust. "That manager guy. He didn't follow us. He ran back into the office."

"He must have been crazy, Mister Scott."

"No. He knew what he was doing. He was sane enough to warn us to run for our lives first. But the poor devil wouldn't have stood a chance."

They got to their feet. Scott's neck was stinging and when he put his hand to it he felt the tackiness of half-congealed blood. He smiled tightly. A small price to pay for an almost miraculous escape.

Now the danger was over, people were appearing in the square, converging slowly on the ruins of the hotel. It was the only building that had collapsed. Thinking back, Scott realised the shock had not been a very severe one, nothing to compare with the two major shocks that had devastated the city soon after he arrived in Thunderbird One. But the hotel had been in such a dangerous condition from those early shocks that even a violent tremor had been sufficient to bring it down.

A man in a braided blue uniform joined them as they approached the ruins. Scott recognised the doorman who had tried to stop him from going into the hotel. The man's swarthy face was ghastly pale, and he was trembling visibly.

"*Sacramento!*" he gasped. "If I had not fled when the earth shook…"

Scott's professional instinct now took charge as his senses returned to normal. He caught the man by the arm.

"Was there anybody inside apart from the manager?" he demanded.

"No, señor. The authorities ordered everyone out till the building could be inspected. But Señor Gonzales - the manager - what happened to him?"

Scott gestured at the ruins. "I guess he's in there. He must have been in the office when the building collapsed. It's a million to one chance against him surviving."

"Listen, Mister Scott," Parker broke in, clutching his arm. "Can you hear something? Like someone calling?"

Scott moved to the foot of the vast mound of dirt, masonry and jagged beams and listened carefully. Then he heard it. Someone was crying faintly for help, somewhere deep down beneath the rubble.

He turned to the doorman.

"If it's the manager, he's below street level," he said. "What's down there?"

"A cellar, señor."

"Could he have been pushed into it from his office?"

"It is possible, señor. If the floor collapsed he would fall into the cellar."

Scott switched on his radio. "Mobile control from Scott. Can you read me?"

"Scott from mobile control," replied Virgil's voice. "Come in, Scott. Have you found Lady Penelope?"

"No. But we've got another rescue chore." He gave Virgil the location. "Get over here fast with the Mole, Virgil. Leave Gordon in charge there."

"F.A.B., I'm on my way Scott."

Police had now arrived on the scene and the doorman was explaining excitedly to an officer. With screeching siren a mobile rescue squad raced round the square and halted.

Scott went to meet the commander. At sight of the International Rescue uniform the woman was respectful.

"Be careful how you tackle this, señora," Scott said, after telling her about the manager. "The way I see it he's probably trapped in a pocket down there. One hasty move and tons of masonry may crash down on him."

"What do you suggest?"

"Try to get a microphone probe to him and a light. He may be able to give you the low-down on the situation."

"Si, señor."

The woman turned away, giving brisk orders to her squad. Scott watched anxiously as they located the buried man's approximate position with a direction finder and then began to work slowly towards it, proceeding carefully through the debris with a probe bearing a hypersensitive microphone.

Presently Parker caught Scott's arm.

"Wot about 'er Ladyship?" he asked. "Couldn't we leave this to Mister Virgil and these blokes and try to get on 'er trail, sir?"

Scott smiled at him. "Guess I know how you feel about her, Parker. But we'll see this through first. That guy down there may be able to help us. I think you were right about him. He knew more than he was prepared to tell us."

"You mean he was in with them blokes wot attacked me and 'er Ladyship?"

"I wouldn't go so far as to say that, but I've got a hunch he knew something."

There was a shout from the squad commander, and Scott went to her.

"We are through to him, señor," she said eagerly. "He says he is hurt badly. The heavy safe in his office fell through the floor with him and he is trapped under it by a beam. But the safe is keeping the debris from falling on him. It has saved his life."

"Let me talk to him." Scott took the microphone and spoke into it. "This is International Rescue. Can you hear me, Señor Gonzales?"

"Si, si. I hear you, señor." The trapped man's voice was hoarse with pain and terror. "You—you will help me—please?"

"Just take it easy. Everything's going to be all right. You say the safe is protecting you? How?"

"It is leaning against the wall, like the side of a tent, señor."

"Does it look firmly wedged?"

"It is only resting against the wall. If it should slide…"

Señor Gonzales said no more, but Scott got the picture. The slightest tremor might cause that heavy safe to slide down the wall and crush the helpless man which for the moment it was shielding from the great weight of rubble above.

"Where are you hurt?" Scott asked.

"There is great pain inside me, señor. And my leg. I think it is broken."

"Okay. Now just hold on. We'll have you out of there as soon as we can."

Scott handed the microphone back to the squad commander.

"Get a stimulant down to him and pain reliever. But don't overdo the drug. We'll need his co-operation. The slightest miscalculation on our part and that safe may crash down on him."

Scott glanced across the plaza to where the headbeams of the Mole had appeared.

"Concentrate on maintaining contact with Señor Gonzales," he went on, "and leave the rest to International Rescue."

"I shall be happy to do so, señor," the woman said earnestly. She gave Scott a plan. "Perhaps you will find this useful, señor. It shows the make-up of the soil below us and the position of the mains services."

"Thanks."

The crowd made way for the Mole and it came to rest a few yards from where the rescue workers were busy at the pilot bore hole in the light of arc lamps and vehicle headlights.

"What's the drill, Scott?" asked Virgil, opening the hatch of the machine and looking out at his brother.

Scott briefed him on the situation. "I guess if we try to dig down to that guy we might cause a subsidence, Virgil. I suggest you bore in from the side. The base of the cellar walls is built against solid rock. Better take this plan."

Virgil took the plan and scanned it quickly.

"That's okay. I'll tunnel from the other side of the road to avoid the electricity conduits and the sewer. Be seeing you."

The hatch closed. The motors whined and the crowd parted again as the weird boring machine turned and glided across the road into the shrubbery where Scott and Parker had sheltered not long before.

"Do you think it can make it, Mister Scott?" asked Parker anxiously as they watched the tail of the machine tilt upwards, then the point of the screw nose dig into the soft soil.

"I've never seen anything the Mole couldn't get through yet, Parker," Scott said. "That drill head is made of a special alloy of Brains' own invention. It's harder than diamonds. It'll make it all right. The question is; will it make it in time?"

The crowd gaped in silent wonder as the Mole bored rapidly into the soft earth. Then it was gone and there was only a neat round hole with hard packed sides to mark its going.

Once beneath the surface, Virgil had to steer blind by means of his sensitive instruments. These registered the slightest change in density of the soil through which he was boring, and detected obstructions such as sewers, gas or electricity mains. For the moment he knew he had nothing to fear from them, for already he was well below their level, boring steadily downwards at a sharp angle towards the solid rock. Behind the Mole, concrete solution was being pumped through ducts to seal the walls of the bore hole.

But there were other hazards that Virgil tried not to think about. In earthquake country rock faults were constantly shifting. If a shift occurred at the precise moment when the Mole was boring through it, the machine would be snapped like a brittle stick and he would be trapped in a tomb of rock from which he would be lucky to be rescued before his air supplies ran out. Maybe it was a hundred to one chance, but it was there.

He struck the rock strata. The nose bit home with a screeching noise that penetrated the stout hull of the machine and set it vibrating. He watched his gauges carefully. There was a critical temperature for even the tough metal of the screw head. Once that was reached it was dangerous to go on at the same speed, for the nose might fuse solid to the rock.

Slowly the Mole levelled out and churned its way through the rock, passing several feet below the mains conduits and below the sewer. Virgil elevated a little, aiming to come into the cellar from the side rather than from below.

Presently he stopped the motor and used the seismicrobe, sounding for the cellar. The reading showed it was less than twenty feet ahead of him.

He triggered the motor again, then went on slowly, steadily, foot by foot. He had to be careful now so that earth vibrations set up by the machine did not cause the precariously balanced safe to fall.

He stopped again, and spoke into his microphone.

"Scott from Mole. Now ten feet from target. What's the position there?"

"Mole from Scott. Good going, Virgil. Hold it. I'll check." After a moment Scott went on, "Position's much as before, but Gonzales is getting weaker. He says dirt is trickling down the wall. He can feel your vibrations."

"That's what I'm afraid of, Scott."

"We've got to take the risk, Virgil. It'll take hours to get down to him manually from the top, and even then we couldn't be certain the safe wouldn't fall before we got to him. Go on slowly and maintain open circuit."

"F.A.B., Scott."

Virgil crawled on. Nine feet . . . eight . . . seven . . . six. . . . Each foot seemed to take an hour to cover, yet it was only a matter of seconds.

He stopped again to check with Scott.

"More dirt falling," his brother reported. "Guess the poor devil's half dead with fright. Those last five feet are going to seem like five years to him."

"And to me," Virgil replied grimly. "Here goes."

The motor whined again. The screw bit greedily into the solid rock, inching the machine forward.

An eternity seemed to pass. Virgil kept his eyes glued to his meter dials. The last foot was the most dangerous of all. If he did not cut cleanly through, if he caused the wall of the cellar to crumble and collapse, the disturbance might bring the safe and tons of rubble above it down on the unfortunate Gonzales.

In spite of the air conditioning, sweat stood out on his tense face. He sucked in his breath sharply as the pitch of the screw's whine changed suddenly, and a needle flickered violently.

The point of the screw was through.

Abruptly he cut the motor. In the silence that clamped down on the machine he could hear his own heart thudding.

"Break through," he said hoarsely into the microphone. "What's the position?"

"Gonzales thinks the safe slipped an inch or two. He can't be sure. He's getting very weak. Virgil!"

"Yes?"

"I don't think you'd better risk going into the cellar. Reverse to the surface."

"But—"

"Do as I say, Virgil. I'll make a manual rescue. It will only take a few minutes longer and it'll be much safer."

"For Gonzales, maybe, but not for you, Scott."

"Don't waste time arguing," his brother said with a note of authority. "Get back here. That's an order, Virgil."

"F.A.B.!"

Slowly Virgil reversed the Mole, back through the solid rock and then up through the softer strata where the concrete solution had sealed the tunnel into a smooth passage.

When the machine reached the surface, Scott was waiting in borrowed overalls, helmet with headlamp and rescue equipment.

Virgil opened the hatch. "Now look here, Scott," he said determinedly, "if any guy's going to risk his neck, it's me."

But Scott had already gone, paying out the rope and telephone line behind him.

He shot feet first down the sharply sloping borehole until it levelled out. Then he ran along bent double, racing against time.

It didn't take him long to cover the thirty feet to the wall of the cellar and presently his headlamp picked out the hole the screw had pierced in it. It was large enough to take him.

He peered through, flashing his powerful lamp around. He saw that the Mole had penetrated the wall close to the floor at a spot which was comparatively free from debris. Looking up, he saw the reason why. Two of the floor joists were jammed across from wall to wall a couple of feet above his head, forming a platform on which fallen masonry had lodged.

To his left he saw the big green safe.

It was canted at an angle of about forty-five degrees, with

one bottom edge resting on the debris on the cellar floor, the corresponding top edge resting against the wall. Beneath it, held down by a massive floor beam which was jammed beneath the safe, was the limp, dust-covered figure of Señor Gonzales. The lamp that had been lowered to him had fallen from his hand.

He appeared unconscious, but as Scott wormed through the hole and crawled towards him, the man's eyes flickered open and lit up eagerly.

"Señor!" he gasped. "You - you come to save me?"

"Sure," Scott said. "Just relax. Everything's going to be okay."

"But the safe, I am sure it is still slipping. Listen!"

Dirt streamed down the wall behind them and Scott's heart leapt as he heard an ominous grating sound.

"Nothing to worry about," he lied, forcing himself to speak calmly. "That safe's as firm as the rock of Gibraltar. Now hold on while I get you out of here. It may hurt a little."

"I-I can stand it, señor, but please to be quick."

Scott was conscious of a movement behind him and saw another figure in overalls crawl through the hole in the wall. In the light of the beam he recognised Virgil.

"I thought I told you to—"

"Quit arguing, Scott. I'm here. Two heads and two pairs of hands are better than one. I brought a jack. Figured you might need it."

"Sure. We can't shift this beam off him with the weight of the safe holding it down. I'll have to saw through it. Better jack it up on the other side so it doesn't fall on him."

Scott got the saw from his rescue kit. Sweat streaming round his ribs, he worked as fast as he dared without putting too much pressure on the beam. A laser cutter would have been quicker, but there would have been too great a risk of fire.

By the time he was through the beam, Gonzales was unconscious. Scott and Virgil eased him from under the safe and got him through the hole into the tunnel. Only then dared they breathe freely again.

The rescue squad commander was waiting with a stretcher. They roped the unconscious man to it, then hauled him gently to the surface, where a doctor and an ambulance were waiting.

A cheer went up from the crowd as they appeared.

The doctor made a quick examination of Gonzales and shook her head gravely.

"We may be just in time," she said, giving an injection. "There are internal injuries."

As Gonzales was being lifted into the ambulance he opened his eyes.

"The...the brave señor who saved me," he gasped. "The International Rescue señor. I-I must speak to him."

Scott went to the man's side. Pain was causing sweat to bead on his dust-grimed face. He clutched Scott's arm.

"You are a very brave man, señor. I thank you. But there is something I must tell you. You ask me about Señor Creighton-Ward and the young señorita who come to inquire about him. The señorita I know nothing about, but the señor..."

He broke off, his face contorting with pain, and the doctor said urgently to Scott, "Do not be long with him, señor, or your courage will have been in vain."

"No, wait, please!" Gonzales begged. "I must finish. It is on my conscience. Señor, in the safe is a bag, a pigskin bag with a draw-string which Señor Creighton-Ward gave me to keep for him. When the tremor came I went to my office to get it. I...I was going to steal it. I have been punished for my sin. That bag, señor, it may hold the key to a great fortune..."

His voice trailed away and he fell back unconscious again. At a sign from the doctor the ambulance men slid the stretcher into the vehicle and the doors were shut.

"What did he say, Scott?" asked Virgil, as the ambulance drove off.

Scott told him.

"Whatever it is in that safe," he added, "it may throw some light on what's happened to Lady Penelope and her cousin. Where's Parker?"

Scott glanced round just in time to see the butler scurrying through the bushes towards the borehole, carrying a rescue helmet.

"What's he up to?" Virgil asked.

Parker stopped at the hole, strapped on the helmet, then sat down and put his feet into the mouth of the borehole.

"Hey, come back, you idiot!" Scott shouted, running towards him.

But before he could reach him, Parker had disappeared.

Scott didn't hesitate. He dived headfirst into the hole and shot down the tunnel in pursuit. When he reached the bottom of the slope, he saw a bobbing light ahead. He got to his feet and, crouching, raced after Parker, yelling to him to stop, but the man ignored him.

By the time Scott reached the hole leading into the cellar, Parker was at the door of the tilted safe, his hand on the tumbler dial, his ear against it.

Scott scrambled through to his side.

"You crazy fool," he gasped. "The whole caboodle's likely to fall any minute—"

"Quiet please, guv," Parker said calmly. "I can't 'ear what I'm a-doin'."

"But—"

"Shaddup!" Parker growled with a fierce glare. "This may be our only clue to 'er Ladyship."

Scott fell silent, wondering at the courage and devotion of this ex-crook who was prepared to risk his life in the hope of finding a clue to the whereabouts of his vanished mistress.

But Scott forgot the danger as he crouched there, watching in fascination while Parker twirled the dial, his craggy face intent. There was no sound but the clicking of the tumblers and the creaking of straining timber somewhere above them.

A stream of dirt trickled onto Parker's side-turned face, but he ignored it.

The seconds ticked away. Behind Scott, Virgil appeared in the hole.

"Hey, what the—?"

Scott gestured for silence, and at that moment Parker gave a cry of satisfaction.

"Got it! The crib's cracked!"

He turned the handle and the massive door swung open. He shone his headlamp inside, then reached in and brought out a pigskin bag with a draw-string, to which was attached a label.

"'Señor Creighton-Ward'," he read. "Guess this is it."

A timber groaned and a shower of debris fell on them.

"Lumme," he grinned at the brothers. "I think we'd better 'op it quick before the roof falls in."

Scott bundled the others through the hole and crawled out after them. He'd gone scarcely three yards along the tunnel when there was a crash back in the cellar and dust billowed down the tunnel to set him coughing and spluttering.

"A fool of a risk to take," he muttered. "Let's hope it's been worth it."

When they reached the surface, Parker handed the bag to Scott.

"You'd better see what's in it, guv."

Scott opened the bag and stared in amazement as he drew from it a cord about two feet long made of different coloured threads twisted together. From it smaller threads of different colours, knotted at intervals, hung like a fringe.

"What the heck!" Virgil gasped. "You mean to say you guys risked your lives for a bit of string?"

"Pardon, señors," said a quiet voice behind them.

They turned to see a young police captain in white uniform smiling at them.

She took the strange cord from Scott and examined it.

"Señors, this is not just a bit of string as you think. It is a *quipu*. The ancient Incas used them to keep records, just as we keep account books. Some of them are of great historical interest."

Scott frowned. Lady Penelope's cousin must have deposited the *quipu* in the hotel safe because he valued it. And what had Gonzales said? The bag might hold the key to a great fortune.

But how could he discover the significance of this *quipu* as the police captain called it?

As if the young officer had read his thoughts, she said, "Professor Carlos de Sabata is a great authority on the *quipu*, señor. He will be pleased to tell you about this one."

"Where can I find him?"

"In the Hacienda del Caldo in the village of San Pedro, señor. He has a museum there."

"Thanks."

"You are welcome, señor. I am happy to be of service. You have done much for us."

The captain clicked her heels and saluted with a smile, then went away.

Virgil looked curiously at Scott.

"You're not thinking of getting this thing translated?"

"Why not? As Parker said when he was sticking his neck out down in that cellar, this may be our only clue as to what's happened to Lady Penelope. I wouldn't like him to think he'd taken that risk for nothing."

"You're blinkin' right, Mister Scott," growled Parker. "If you don't go and see that professor bloke, I'll go meself. I ain't leavin' here till I've done something about findin' her Ladyship."

"Neither am I, Parker. But I'll have to check with Dad first. Let's get back to mobile control."

Virgil returned to the Mole, and Scott and Parker hurried across the square to the avenue that led to the main plaza.

From the shadows, the Hood, dressed as a member of the rescue squad, removed his helmet and goggles and grinned evilly.

"So the *quipu* is of great value," he muttered. "Perhaps it leads to the treasure that the cousin of our International Rescue lady was seeking? I think I shall prepare a little surprise for Mister Scott Tracy."

CHAPTER SIX

HACIENDA TRAP

In the light of the airport arc lamps and auxiliary flares the huge green shape of Thunderbird Two settled down on its hydraulic stilts over the pod containing the Mole and the Firefly.

It was just like a broody hen settling down on an egg that it was about to hatch, Scott thought, as he watched from behind his mobile equipment in the jeep.

Thunderbird One, standing on its landing gear on the next runway, cast a long shadow across its sister craft.

Beyond the perimeter of the landing field, a crowd of onlookers was being held back by barriers, police and airport guards in response to Scott's insistence on maximum security precautions to prevent the photographing of International Rescue equipment.

"Mobile control from Thunderbird Two," came Virgil's voice over the radio. "Ready to launch."

"F.A.B.," Scott said. "Bon voyage. Be seeing you when I've tied up this Lady Penelope business."

"Okay, Scott. If you want any help, let us know and we'll be with you in an hour. So long!"

The jets roared. Thunderbird Two rolled forward, and its nose lifted. Then it took off with an effortless ease that seemed incredible in view of its great size, and vanished into the darkness beyond the lake of light that marked the airport.

The thunder of the jets faded rapidly as it hurtled out over the moonlit Pacific, and presently there was silence, broken only by the excited talk of the sightseers beyond the barriers.

Scott contacted base and his father's rugged face appeared on the monitor screen before him.

"Scott to base. Thunderbird Two away, Dad," he reported.

"Okay, son," Jeff said. "Now you know what you've got to do?"

"Sure. Find Lady Penelope."

"There's more to it than that, son. You've got to find her before that guy Hood makes her talk. She doesn't know many of our technical secrets, but she knows the biggest secret of all - the location of our island base."

"He won't find her an easy nut to crack, Dad."

"Guess not, but everyone's got a breaking point, Scott. Lady Penelope may be tough, but," Jeff's face tightened grimly, "the thought of her suffering…"

"Don't worry too much, Dad," Scott broke in. "I'm not so sure that guy *has* got her."

"What makes you say that?"

"Well, coshing Parker to get her doesn't seem like the Hood. Why didn't he just use the hypnotic power of his eyes to knock Parker out? Why employ a gang of thugs? It's my hunch someone else has snatched her."

"Who'd want to do that?"

"I don't know. But it could be someone who knew who she was. They might figure a woman like Penelope would command a mighty big ransom."

"Just plain kidnappers, huh? Could be, son. In a way I hope so. Guess she'd get better treatment from them, if they're hoping to make some money out of her, than from that Hood guy. He's as ruthless as a man-eating tiger. Okay, Scott! Get cracking."

As Scott signed off he saw Lady Penelope's Rolls-Royce gliding across the tarmac. Parker had been to fetch it from where he had parked it outside the earthquake-racked town.

Parker helped him to load the mobile equipment into Thunderbird One. The hatch was shut and sealed. Only Scott would be able to open it again. At a sign from him, a guard of police moved into position around it. Thankful for what International Rescue had done, the city authorities were falling over themselves to comply with every request Scott made.

"Now we'll go and see Professor de Sabata," Scott said, as he and Parker walked to the Rolls. "It's a long shot, but that *quipu* may hold some clue to Lady Penelope's disappearance."

"By the way, Mister Scott," said Parker, taking an envelope from his pocket. "'Ere's a picture of the 'onourable Gus wot 'er Ladyship had in the car. It might come in 'andy if we've got to look for 'im as well as 'er Ladyship."

"Sure might…" Scott checked as he looked at the

photograph Parker had handed him. "Say, I've seen this guy before."

And then he remembered where. This was the young fair-haired Englishman whom he had seen carried from the ruins of the restaurant just before the second big 'quake had shattered the city. He remembered the man muttering in his semi-consciousness, "*I must tell Penny.*" The name had been of no significance to him then.

"No wonder that guy's face seemed familiar," he said aloud. "He's mighty like Lady Penelope herself."

Parker regarded him curiously. "You've seen the gentleman, Mister Scott?"

"Sure." Scott told him where. "Drive me to the control building, Parker. Better see if I can trace where that fellow was taken. A word with him might help plenty."

"Righto, sir. 'Op in."

When the Rolls stopped at the control building, Scott went in and spoke to the communications officer.

"Si, señor!" the woman said. "It should be easy enough to find out where a particular casualty was taken. Rescue Control keep a record. I will check."

A few moments later the woman smiled round at him. "Santa Anna hospital, señor. Shall I get you a line?"

"Please."

Scott took the receiver and was presently speaking to the hospital superintendent.

"Señor Creighton-Ward?" the voice at the other end said. "Yes, he was brought in yesterday suffering from mild concussion, associated with amnesia."

"He's lost his memory? Is he well enough to have a visitor? I'd like to talk to him."

"I am afraid that's impossible, señor."

"You mean he's still unconscious?"

"No - he was discharged a few hours ago. A friend called and asked if he could take care of him. We were only too happy. You appreciate, señor, that we need every available bed, and apart from the amnesia, which will probably pass of its own accord, there was nothing seriously wrong with the Englishman."

"Sure. I understand that. Have you got the name and address of this friend of Señor Creighton-Ward?"

There was a silent pause, and then the official said, "Apparently it was not taken. In the confusion - we are being rushed off our feet, you understand? - no one seems to have taken it. The gentleman was merely told to bring the patient back if there were complications. I am sorry, señor."

"That's okay," Scott said. "Thank you."

But Scott's face was grim when he returned to the car.

"Wot's wrong, guv?" Parker asked.

Scott told him what he had learned, and went on, "I sure don't like the smell of this, Parker. We know Gus didn't return to the hotel. It's my hunch that was no friend who picked him up."

"You mean he was kidnapped, sir, like 'er Ladyship?"

"Sure. By the same guys I guess." Scott settled into the rear seat. "Let's go and see that professor. He may be our only hope now."

The Rolls glided from the airport, through an avenue of people kept back by police, and swung north, bypassing the city with its blocked streets.

The mist that had hung over the countryside all day had lifted now, and outside the city with its drifting pall of dust and smoke the air was clear. Above the skyline of the Andes the Moon was climbing into a star-flecked blue-black sky.

Parker drove carefully, the car's powerful headbeams stabbing twin cones of vivid yellow-white light through the darkness ahead. Here and there gigantic slabs of concrete had been thrust up by the force of the earthquake, but only in one place did they find the highway completely blocked. A gang was at work in the light of arc lamps, clearing it.

A temporary track had been bulldozed through a hill slope to bypass the obstruction, and once they were past that they met no more delays.

They were in bed-rock country now, and earthquakes had little effect on this sort of terrain unless they were exceptionally severe.

Presently a signpost flashed in the headlight like a ghostly finger pointing to the left, and Scott saw the name San Pedro.

Parker swung off the main highway and they found themselves on what was little more than a hard-packed dirt track, climbing the foothills of the Andes.

They passed no other traffic. Behind and below them the lights of Lima glowed like stars against the darkness of the coastal strip. Here and there a light in a farmer's dwelling pierced the gloom beside the road. There was no other sign of life.

In spite of the urgency of their mission Parker still drove carefully, for they could never tell if the road ahead might be broken by a fissure opened up by the earthquake.

But at last they saw the lights of a village, and presently the white walls of the house appeared in the moonlight.

There was no one on the single street. Inside the cantina shadows moved against a blind. But the Hacienda del Caldo was not difficult to find, for the signpost pointed up a winding track to where a long white single-storied house stood against the dark hill slope.

The gates of the hacienda were open. Gravel crunched under the wheels of the car as Parker drove slowly up the curving drive between fragrant smelling trees and shrubs and brought it to a standstill at the foot of a short flight of steps leading up to a long wide veranda.

In the house a single light showed from the glass entrance door. But, although the car's approach must have been heard, no one appeared.

Scott got out. A cold breeze seeping down from the mountains stirred the undergrowth.

He froze, looking about him warily. He had the sensation of being watched. Had they been followed?

A night bird screeched among the trees. A bat flitted across the face of the Moon. But that feeling persisted.

"Parker," he said softly. "Come up with me and wait outside. I've got a feeling there may be trouble."

"Right you are, guv."

Parker took a gun and a round small object from a dashboard packet. He slipped them into his jacket, then got out. The gullwing doors of the Rolls closed behind Parker. Scott knew that nothing short of a laser beam could gain entrance to the car now.

Slowly he mounted the steps to the veranda, his hand going instinctively to the machine pistol in the blue holster at his side. It was ready loaded with the yellow barrel containing knock-out darts. He and his brothers never used lethal bullets unless there was no other choice.

When they reached the veranda, Scott approached the glass door, while Parker faded into the shadows beside it, putting his back against the wall and watching the moonlit shadowy grounds about the car.

Scott pulled a chain that hung beside the door, wondering once again why no one had appeared at the sound of the car's approach.

Somewhere in the depths of the silent house a bell jangled eerily. For a few moments nothing happened. Scott was about to ring again when he became conscious of a faint humming sound.

He looked up. He could see nothing in the shadows above him, but he got the impression that an unseen eye was watching him. A television camera, he thought, feeding a closed circuit, so that a caller could be viewed from inside the house before being admitted.

It was a common enough precaution in the world these days, he told himself, but perhaps doubly essential in an isolated hacienda like this at the edge of a wild country that had changed little in centuries.

The humming became louder. Electronic bolts slid back and the door glided sideways. Light splashed out on him.

"Come in, my friend," said a voice.

Scott motioned to Parker to remain on guard, and entered.

He found himself in a long narrow hall with white painted walls and dark oak floor, on which bright Indian rugs were scattered. It was lighted by imitation antique lamps. The few articles of furniture were dark and heavy, centuries old, he thought. On the walls hung ancient weapons that might have been used by the Conquistadores who had conquered Peru for Spain, and grotesquely carved ceremonial masks of native workmanship.

A man emerged from a doorway along the hall. He was powerfully built, with a mane of greying hair and a goatee beard. He was dressed in a white linen suit and wore horn-rimmed spectacles with very thick lenses.

"Welcome, señor," he said, smiling as he came forward. "It is an honour to meet a member of International Rescue. You have done so much for my poor countrymen in their hour of need."

"It's been a pleasure, Professor de Sabata," Scott smiled.

He glanced round as he heard the door slide softly into place behind him.

"You must excuse my caution, señor," the other man said. "It is lonely here. My servants are down in Lima looking for their families lost in the earthquake. Sometimes in the hills there are desperate men. And I have much treasure here."

"Treasure?"

"Valuable relics of our country's great history. I have a museum."

"Sure. The police officer who recommended me to call on you mentioned you had a museum. You are a great authority on the ancient Incas, professor?"

"I have acquired a little fame on that subject, my friend." He waved his hand towards the room from which he had just emerged. "But please come into my study."

Scott followed him into a big book-lined room with a desk on which were a telephone and automatic typewriter. Curios stood on shelves. On the wall was a small television screen, in which Scott got a view of the veranda outside the front door, the steps and the Rolls-Royce on the drive below. The professor was about to switch off the screen when Scott stopped him.

"Mind leaving it, professor?" he asked. "I'd like to keep my eye on it. I had a feeling I was being followed here."

"Followed?" The other man blinked at him through his thick lenses. "But who would follow you?"

"I don't know. But I think there may be people interested enough in what I've brought to you to want to get hold of it."

"You intrigue me, my friend. May I see it?"

Scott took from his pocket the pigskin bag containing the *quipu* that Parker had taken from the safe under the ruined hotel.

"I'm told you can read the cord writings of the ancient Incas," he said, taking out the *quipu*. "I'd like to know what this one says, professor."

He looked up to find the other man gazing eagerly at the *quipu*. There was a strange glint in the eyes behind the thick lenses. He held his hand out.

"Let me look at it, Señor Tracy," he said, a harsh note in his voice.

Scott's eyes narrowed suspiciously. He thrust the *quipu* back into his pocket.

"Who told you my name, señor?" he demanded.

The other man laughed shortly and spread his hands. "Why, everyone knows the members of International Rescue."

"That's just what they don't know. Certainly I've told no one in Peru my name."

With a sudden movement, Scott snatched the glasses from the bearded face, and with a snarl of baffled rage the man sprang back, his eyes lighting up like malignant black jewels.

Scott stared incredulously. He had seen those eyes before, but in a different face.

"The man with the glaring eyes!" he growled. "The guy who calls himself Hood."

The Hood's lips writhed viciously. His eyes flashed.

"Give me that *quipu*, Tracy."

Scott knew the strange power of those eyes. They could hypnotise a man into instant unconsciousness. He dared not meet them. He ducked and dived headlong forward. His head rammed home against a barrel chest, and the Hood staggered back against the desk.

Scott followed up, but a vicious hammer of a fist caught him on the temple. Something seemed to explode in his head. He sank to his knees, a wave of nausea sweeping through him. He saw the Hood looming above him and groped for his machine pistol. But, as he clawed it out, a kick sent it flying from his hand.

"Give me that *quipu*, Tracy!" snarled the Hood.

Dimly Scott was aware of the sound of crashing glass; then

something exploded with a dull plop on the floor between him and the other man, and bluish fumes billowed up.

The Hood started back with a cry of alarm. As the gas reached him, he coughed and spluttered. With an angry oath he turned and ran from the room.

Scott scrambled up and, holding his breath, dashed in pursuit. He reached the door of the study in time to see the Hood blast the electronically sealed glass door with a gun then hurtle through it onto the veranda.

Scott, weak from the blow on the temple, was slow to follow, and by the time he reached the veranda there was no sign of his assailant.

A moment later he heard the roar of jets and then from among the trees rose the black bug shape of a heli-jet. A harsh, hate-ridden voice drifted through the night.

"I'll get you, Tracy. Next time you won't be so fortunate, my friend."

For an instant the aircraft was silhouetted against the Moon, and then it was gone.

CHAPTER SEVEN

MESSAGE FROM THE PAST

As the sound of the heli-jet faded into the night, Parker joined Scott on the veranda.

"Who was that bloke, Mister Scott?"

"The guy with the glaring eyes."

Parker stared at him. "You - you mean *he* was the professor?"

"No, Parker. Somehow he must have learned we were coming here and laid a trap for us. He has probably disposed of the real professor. We'd better look for him."

They went back into the house. "You threw that gas bomb?" Scott asked.

"Yes, guv. I was taking a butcher's hook round the place to see if anyone was snoopin' around and I happened to look into the room. There was that bloke threatening you and you down on your knees, so I reckoned I ought to take a 'and. I smashed the winder and chucked the bomb."

"Lucky you did, Parker. He was after that *quipu*. But for your prompt action, I guess he'd have got it."

They opened all the windows, switched on the electric fans to hurry the clearance of gas, then systematically searched the place. But they found no sign of the rightful owner of the hacienda or his servants.

Scott led the way back into the hall. "Maybe the professor wasn't here anyway," Scott said. "He might be down in Lima helping—"

"WAAAAH!"

At Parker's startled yell, Scott swung round to see him disappearing through a hole in the floor where a trap door had opened up. Surprise, shock, fear, were all mingled in Parker's craggy face in the instant it was visible to Scott. Then he had vanished. There was a clattering and a bumping for a few moments and then silence.

His mouth dry, Scott hurried to the open trap, and saw stone steps leading down. A faint light was visible far below and from the depths came a groan.

"Parker!" he yelled. "Are you okay?"

Parker's voice echoed back. "I regret to say I 'ave sustained numerous bruises on the tenderest parts of my anatomy, Mister Scott."

Scott grinned, relieved that the butler seemed to be alright.

"Stand by!" he called. "I'll be right down to pick up the pieces."

He had descended only a few steps when there was a terrified yell from below and the next instant he saw Parker tearing towards him as though his life depended on it.

When the butler reached Scott, he grabbed at his arm, pointing down.

"There - there's a lot of 'orrible mummies down there, Mister Scott!" he gasped.

"Mummies?"

"Yes. Blokes wot 'ave been dead for 'undreds of years, all sitting up in 'oles round the wall, grinning something awful at me. I ain't afraid of nothin' that's flesh and blood, but—"

"Take it easy, Parker," Scott grinned. "If they've been dead as long as you say, they can't be very dangerous. Let's take a closer look."

Parker swallowed. "Okay, Mister Scott. I-I'll be right behind you."

Scott descended slowly. The steps curved slightly near the bottom, and as he turned the bend he saw the light coming from a naked electric bulb hanging from the stone ceiling of what appeared to be a long vault.

He went down a few more steps, then halted. He had been amused by Parker's fear but now he felt an icy prickling at the base of his skull.

In niches round the wall sat mummies black with age, wearing hideous death masks and shrouded in cloths of various colours.

"Wot did I tell you, Mister Scott?" Parker whispered hoarsely in his ear. "It's a charnel 'ouse, that's wot it is. A chamber of 'orrors - *oh, no!!*"

"What's wrong now, Parker?" Scott asked, glancing round at him curiously.

Parker, his eyes wide, his face drained of colour, was pointing with a shaking finger to one side of the vault.

"Th-there's one of 'em c-coming to life," he gulped.

Scott followed the direction of his pointing finger and again he felt that icy prickling down his spine. From the shadows a figure was shuffling, wrapped in a dark cloth similar to those of the mummies. It was making a faint moaning sound.

With a spasmodic movement, Parker seemed to get his legs to work and would have fled if Scott hadn't grabbed his arm.

"Hold it, Parker! That's no mummy. It's a man - bound and gagged. My guess is it's the professor."

Warily Parker followed him into the vault to where the figure had collapsed on the floor. Scott saw that he was right. The cloth had fallen from the figure's head revealing the grey-bearded features of a man with plaster stuck across his mouth.

Scott quickly freed him, and helped him to his feet.

"Professor de Sabata?" he asked.

"Si, señor! I am most grateful to you." The man smiled when he saw the insignia on Scott's uniform. "International Rescue. You live up to your name by rescuing me, si!"

"What happened?"

"This man, he comes to the house. He pretends he wishes to consult me and then - his eyes, señor! Never have I seen such eyes. They flashed lights. I cannot look away from them. Something seems to explode in my brain and then I know nothing more until I find myself down here among my mummies. I cannot free myself, but I manage to get to the switch that opens the trap door. I think perhaps my servant when he comes back from Lima will look for me down here."

Scott chuckled and glanced at Parker, who was looking sheepish.

"And you pressed the switch just as my friend stepped on the trap door. I think he's a couple of shades greyer than he was before. All this gave him the fright of his life."

The professor bowed to Parker. "A thousand apologies, señor."

Parker grinned. "Lumme, you wasn't to know, mister." He waved his hand at the mummies. "But this lot's enough to give anyone the creeps. Who are they? Your ancestors?"

"Some of them, perhaps. Who knows? They belong to a race who inhabited Peru even before the Incas came."

Scott told him about the *quipu*.

"The fellow with the glaring eyes is an old enemy of ours!" Scott added. "He must have learned we were coming to see you, got here first and took your place. He tried to get the *quipu*."

"Why should he want it?"

"I don't know. But we were told it might be the key to a great fortune."

The professor frowned. "Let me see it. So many of these *quipus* are but records of stores, of granaries and fields." He broke off as Scott produced the *quipu* and his dark eyes lit up eagerly.

"Señor, this is something very important. I can see that at a glance by the colours of the threads in the cords. It is so well preserved, too. Exceptionally so. But I need my codes to translate it. Let us go upstairs."

"That'll be a pleasure, señor," Parker growled with an uneasy glance at the hideously grinning mummies about him.

Scott told Parker to keep guard outside the house while he followed Professor de Sabata into the study. The professor took a leather-bound book from a shelf and sat down to decipher the cord writing.

Scott watched anxiously. Lady Penelope's fate might depend on the correct translation of this message from the past.

The professor was muttering to himself as he scribbled on a pad before him, but Scott could sense that his interest was now tinged with excitement.

Presently he looked up, his dark eyes gleaming.

"Señor, whoever told you this might hold the key to a great fortune was right. I shall not read it to you, for the language is archaic. But it refers to the legendary emerald mines of the Incas."

"I don't know the legend, professor. Were they valuable?"

"Valuable? It was rumoured they were the richest the world has ever known. Have you not read the story of Pizarro, who conquered Peru from the Incas? It is said that as a peace offering the Emperor of the Incas gave him seven enormous emeralds which had come from these mines. Pizarro said they were the real treasure of the Incas. *'Give me their emeralds,'* he told his private priest, *'and you can have their gold.'"*

"Did Pizarro find the mines?"

"No, señor. The priest tortured and murdered hundreds, perhaps thousands of Incas in trying to find the location of the mines, but he did not succeed. And no one has found them since, although there have been countless expeditions."

"A well-guarded secret, huh?"

"A secret that would have been known to few in the first place, señor; the Inca emperor and a few trusted members of the royal family, all of whom were killed by the Spaniards."

"But this *quipu* tells where the mines are, professor?"

"No, señor. It tells where there is a clue to the location of the mines. It says it is in an Inca temple in their ancient capital of Cuzco. But of course it may not be there after six hundred years."

"This is beginning to sound like a jigsaw puzzle, professor." Scott said.

With an effort he dragged his mind away from thoughts of the fabulous mines and went back to the real object of his visit to the hacienda. He told the professor about the disappearance of Lady Penelope and her cousin, and his hope that the *quipu* might reveal some clue to what had happened to them.

The professor pulled thoughtfully at his beard. "Of course, señor, if the desperados who appear to have kidnapped your friends should know what the *quipu* says—"

"You mean they might have a copy?"

"It is possible. Someone may have seen this before it passed into the hands of Señor Creighton-Ward."

Scott felt that was as good a line to follow as any when he was groping in the dark. He got up.

"Can I leave that *quipu* in your custody for now, professor? I know it will be in safe keeping."

"I shall be honoured, my friend. But first I will make you a copy of the translation in case you need it. It will not take long."

"Thanks. While you're doing that, I'll contact my headquarters and report what you've told me."

Scott left the house. Parker was still patrolling the veranda.

"No sign of that Hood guy coming back?" asked Scott.

"No, guv. I reckon—" Parker broke off, looking down

at the Rolls on the drive below. From it was coming an urgent bleeping. "That's the radio. It's 'er Ladyship's h'emergency call sign."

Parker took the steps four at a time, Scott at his heels. He operated the secret switch that opened the doors and the canopy, and slid into the driving seat, jabbing at the radio button.

"FAB 1 'ere," he said breathlessly. "Parker speaking. Is that you, m'lady?"

"It is, Parker." The calm voice floated into the car in the stillness of the night. "I regret to say I am communicating with you under considerable difficulty. They did not realise that my wristwatch was a radio transmitter, but they may do so if they overhear me."

Scott gestured to Parker and took over the microphone.

"Listen, Lady Penelope," he said urgently, "Scott here. Where are you?"

"In a truck, somewhere on the road to Cuzco. We've been travelling for some hours now, so we may be very near it."

"Is Gus with you?"

"Yes."

"Why were you kidnapped?"

"Evidently they believe poor Gus has the secret to some Inca treasure. They found something they call a *quipu* on him. It looks like a lot of knotted cords. They aren't certain whether it's genuine. They've tried to make Gus speak, but he appears to have lost his memory. He doesn't even know me, but of course he may be putting on an act to stall them."

"That explains why they kidnapped Gus, but why you?"

"Somehow they found out we were related. I have a suspicion that if he doesn't talk they may get rather rough with me to force him to talk—oh!"

With a startled gasp, she went off the air.

"Sounds like they tumbled to what she was doing, Mister Scott," Parker growled.

"Yes. But she's put us in the picture, Parker. They're making for Cuzco, evidently following that *quipu* trail to the lost emerald mines. With a stake like that they won't pull their punches. We've got to get after them. Stand by, just in case she comes through again. I'll see if the professor's finished that translation."

Scott ran back to the house and entered the study. The

professor was speaking into the microphone of his autotyper. After a moment or so he finished and ripped the paper from the machine.

"Here you are, my friend."

"Thanks, professor," Scott said. "I think we may need this."

When he told him about Lady Penelope's radio call, the professor came to his feet.

"Señor," he said eagerly. "You will please to take me with you, si? Perhaps I can be of assistance to you. From Cuzco the trail of your señorita may lead to other places. You may need the advice of an expert."

Scott smiled. "I'll be mighty glad to have you along, professor. How soon can you be ready to travel?"

"Give me an hour, señor, to make the necessary arrangements. My servants will have returned by then to take charge of the hacienda."

"Okay. I'm going to Lima to pick up my aircraft. I'll send Parker back in the car to collect you."

Scott ran out and leapt into the Rolls. "Back to the airport, Parker."

"Yes, sir."

Knowing the hazards of the road now, Parker returned to Lima far faster than he had come from it. Scott was in a cold sweat as the big car screamed down the hill road.

"Phew!" he gasped when the car finally swung through the airport entrance. "Give me Thunderbird One any time. Five thousand miles an hour up there seems like crawling compared with being in this mobile bomb!"

"'Er Ladyship never complains, sir," Parker said with a grin. "She rather likes the h'exhilaration."

"She would," Scott smiled as, with a sighing of air brakes, the car stopped in the shadow of Thunderbird One.

"What's the programme now, sir?" Parker asked.

"I want you to collect the professor and take the main

highway to Cuzco. He'll be your guide. But even at the speed you drive you've got no chance of overtaking those crooks before they reach Cuzco. So I'm blasting off in Thunderbird One. I can reach Cuzco in a few minutes."

"And then?"

"I'll play my cards as they're dealt to me, Parker. If I'm in Cuzco when they arrive I'll have the edge on them. But first I've got to identify them, which may take time. If I can't tackle them alone, I'll try to stall them somehow until you arrive."

"Okey doke!" Parker grinned. "Be seein' you, Mister Scott. But I'm 'oping you can't 'andle 'em alone. I got a score to settle with them blokes."

As Parker swung the car and sent it screaming back across the airfield, Scott opened the hatch of the superjet and climbed into the control cabin. He fired the under jet and slowly the big craft rose into the darkness.

At five hundred feet he cut the under jet, retracted the wings and sent the plane southwards at cruising speed. Switching on the radio he contacted base, and reported briefly to his father the events of the last few hours.

"Smart work, son," Jeff said approvingly. "But too bad you couldn't grab that Hood guy. He'll be on your tail again."

"He's not likely to have anything to touch Thunderbird One, Dad. And if my luck holds, maybe I can rescue Lady Penelope and her cousin long before that guy even knows I'm in Cuzco."

"Sure hope so. There's nothing we can do from this end to help you right now, so watch your step. Good luck!"

"F.A.B.!"

Scott signed off, triggered the motors, and at a thousand miles an hour screamed through the night, climbing steeply to where the snow-capped peaks of the Andes gleamed in the moonlight.

CHAPTER EIGHT

INCA CAPITAL

Fifteen minutes after leaving Lima, Scott saw the lights of Cuzco against the blackness of the mountains. He cut his speed and extended the wings, reflecting with a smile that Parker by now would scarcely have left the hacienda with the professor.

The journey by the main highway was probably nearer five hundred miles than the three hundred-odd he had flown. Even at the speed of the Rolls on a good road, it was going to take all of three hours for Parker to reach Cuzco. And that did not allow for hold-ups such as rock falls brought about by the earthquake.

Centuries ago, Pizarro and his conquistadores had taken weeks to cover the same distance.

In spite of his concern for Lady Penelope and her cousin, Scott was conscious of his pulses racing at the thought that he was on the trail of treasure that had eluded even the rapacious hands of the conquerors of Peru.

Bringing his mind back to the task of navigating, he reduced his speed to a hundred miles an hour and cruised in a wide circle about the ancient city, seeking with his instruments for a place to land.

Just south of the city was a modern airport with brightly lighted runways. He heard the radio control buzzing him, asking him to identify himself, but he ignored it and flew on.

He did not want to reveal his identity. If the men who had kidnapped Lady Penelope were already in the city, the arrival of one of the famous Thunderbirds would alert them. His best chance of rescuing Lady Penelope and her cousin was to arrive in the city unheralded and as an ordinary person.

He found a landing place in an ancient stone quarry about a mile to the east outside the city, where the aircraft would be safe for some hours from curious eyes.

Touching down gently on the level, rubble-coloured bottom where once Inca slaves had toiled, he cut the engines and the silence of the Andean night closed about him.

Above the quarry rim the stars were jewel-bright, almost as bright as they were from the space station, so rarefied was the atmosphere here, over ten thousand feet above sea level.

He switched on the radio and a few moments later Parker's gruff voice said, "Thunderbird One from FAB 1. Can you read me, Mister Scott?"

"Loud and clear. Where are you?"

"We left the 'ouse five minutes ago."

"Good. Has Lady Penelope contacted you again?"

"No, guv. They must have found that radio."

"Guess so. Listen, Parker. I've no means of identifying the truck she said she was a prisoner in. For all I know it may be in the city already. My only chance is to make for the place mentioned in the translation of the *quipu* that the professor made, and hope they turn up there. Tell him I'd like to speak to him."

When the professor came through, Scott studied the copy of the translation and said, "How do I find this temple of Vilca Pata?"

"You will not find it, señor. Only its foundations and the lower stones of the walls still exist. The building erected on the site is now a school. But if the clue to the emerald mines is still hidden there, it is in the vaults which were once the store chambers of the temple."

"Okay. How do I get to it?"

"It is on the right side of the street of El Greco to the south of the great Plaza de Armas where the cathedral is. You cannot miss the plaza, señor. All roads lead to it as they did in the days of the Incas, when it was called Houcay-Pata, the Place of Tears."

"Sounds cheerful," Scott said.

"Place of Blood would have been more suitable, señor."

"Thanks, professor. I'm keeping my fingers crossed that I'll be in time."

In spite of his haste he made his preparations carefully, changing his uniform for a shapeless felt hat and fleecy-lined overall suit that would protect him against the biting cold of the night without making him too conspicuous. Inside the suit he stowed his machine pistol, a torch and a powerful micro-radio transmitter. Then he left the plane, sealing the hatch behind him.

For a moment he stood there, getting his bearings and allowing his lungs to adjust themselves to the rarefied air. Lack of oxygen at these heights could soon sap a man even of his strength if he were not careful.

He did not need to use his wrist compass, for beyond the quarry rim to the west he could see the faint glow of light that marked the position of the ancient capital of the Incas.

Using his torch to pick his way through the rubble of centuries, Scott set off. He found a narrow path cut into the stone wall and climbed it. At the top he paused, getting his breath. Off to his right ran the winding ribbon of road that led north to Lima. Headlights flashed and beamed as vehicles hurtled along it towards the city.

Any one of them, he knew, might be the truck in which Lady Penelope and her cousin were prisoners.

The ground sloped gently towards the city. He made for it, keeping clear of the road, and presently the remains of the old Inca wall loomed up before him, the great stone blocks time-worn and glistening darkly in the moonlight.

He passed through a gap and found himself in a narrow street where adobe buildings had been erected on the dark stone foundations of Inca buildings.

Even in the middle of the twenty-first century the street was as badly lit as any big city slum a hundred and fifty years before. A few naked electric light bulbs were strung on wires between the buildings, and here and there an oil lantern hung outside a door black with age.

In the gloom dim figures, wrapped in blankets against the cold, padded softly past on sandal-shod feet, not giving him a second glance.

He emerged into a wide street and followed it towards the city centre. There were shops here, but most of them were already closed for the night. Ancient cars careered crazily past him with blaring horns, forcing him into doorways. A man in a high-crowned hat and striped poncho shuffled past, leading two heavily laden llamas. Time seemed to have stood still here on the roof of the world.

He came out into the Plaza de Armas. He could not mistake it, for the cathedral which the professor had mentioned towered into the night to silhouette itself against the starry sky.

The plaza was thronged with people. Cantinas were full. The sound of music floated from them, modern pop tunes mingling with age-old plaintive pipings to which the Incas themselves might have listened.

Modern concrete structures jostled Spanish colonial buildings with carved balconies which had been superimposed on Inca ruins. Here, Scott remembered reading, had once stood the fabulous Temple of the Sun whose walls had been coated with gold sheets until stripped by conquerors and melted down with other priceless ornaments and statues. Now it was a convent.

But Scott had no time to linger in this historical place. He made his way round the square to the south side, seeking the street of El Greco.

A dark-skinned police officer in a white uniform glanced curiously at him. He wondered whether he should have sought the cooperation of the local police, but it was unlikely they would be as efficient as down in Lima, and he could not afford to get bogged in a morass of officialdom. Moreover, if the kidnappers thought the police were on their trail they might well dispose of Lady Penelope and her cousin.

He found the street he was looking for, a narrow canyon running down at a steep angle between buildings whose protruding balconies met almost overhead, and as badly lit as the first street he had encountered on entering the town.

The south side, the professor had said. He was about to stop a man to ask him where the school was when he saw it. One of the few lights in the street hung outside a building, and the name of the school was plainly marked on a board fixed beside an iron-studded oak door.

It was an old building, one of the oldest he had seen in the town. The upper half was of brownstone, with a long carved balcony running down the length of it. The lower half was of Inca granite, huge blocks cut perhaps from the very quarry in which he had left Thunderbird One. No light showed from its windows.

Three stone steps led to the massive door, which was recessed between carved stone pillars.

He looked round. There was no one in sight. He darted up the steps into the shadows of the porch and tried the door. He had not really expected it to be open, but to his surprise it yielded at his touch.

He froze, listening. Had the men he was seeking already arrived? Were they in there now, searching?

But he could hear nothing. Gently he eased the door open. Even so a hinge screeched protestingly with a noise that sounded loud enough to wake the ancient dead of the city.

When the opening was wide enough, he squeezed through and carefully closed the door again. He stood there, his back against the wall, staring into the darkness, straining his ears, alert for the slightest indication of danger.

When a man walked with danger as often as Scott, he acquired an animal sense of awareness.

But now Scott sensed nothing. There was only a tiny scampering sound in the darkness. A mouse, he thought.

A faint light from the street came through a window high up. As his eyes gradually adjusted to the gloom, he made out rows of desks. He appeared to be in a large hall.

Scott switched on his torch. In its narrow beam he saw that the walls were panelled in dark oak, and hung with pictures. At the end of the hall was a dais on which stood a big teacher's desk. Behind it was a wall map of South America. To either side of it were closed doors, apparently leading to other parts of the building.

He moved slowly up the hall. If the kidnappers of Lady Penelope were here, he thought there would have been some evidence. He believed they would have left someone on guard.

That door being unlocked had been suspicious, but perhaps the people of Cuzco were honest and there was no more need to lock the schools than there was the churches.

And then a sickening thought struck him. Supposing they had come and gone again, having found what they were seeking? Or suppose they did not come, because the *quipu* they had was not a copy of the original but a fake?

How would he get on the trail of Lady Penelope then?

A little chill went through him. If that *quipu* was a fake, they might try as she had suggested to force the truth out of her cousin by torturing her.

Scott tensed. Behind him a door creaked. He switched off his torch and slowly turned, peering through the gloom towards the door. The thin shaft of light from the lamp outside was widening. He heard the murmur of voices.

Looking about him for a hiding place, Scott saw the teacher's desk and crouched behind it. In the stillness he could hear the thumping of his heart.

Peering above the edge of the desk, he saw a man silhouetted against the light outside as he eased through the partly open door. A man with a high-crowned hat. Another followed him, and another and another until there were four of them standing there just inside the doorway. The hinge creaked again as the door was closed. Instinctively he ducked down, just in time. A torch beam stabbed out, playing around the hall. Again there was a murmur of voices and then booted feet shuffled on the floor as they advanced slowly up the hall between the rows of desks towards his hiding place.

There was a kneehole beneath the desk. Carefully Scott backed into it on his knees. It was a tight fit for one of his size, but it was the only cover available.

The men paused by the dais. A harsh voice said in Spanish, "Which door leads to the vault entrance, Sancho?"

"The left one, Señor Morales. In the teacher's room there are steps under the hearth."

"Bueno. Stay here, Sancho, and keep guard. I don't like that door being unlocked."

"Someone was careless."

"Stay here just the same, Sancho."

"Si, señor."

The men moved away. Scott heard a door open and close. The light of the torch vanished, leaving the hall in darkness. There was silence for a moment, and then the sound of feet shuffling. He heard a chair pulled back. A moment later a match flared.

Scott eased himself out of the kneehole and peered above the desk. A cigarette glowed in the gloom and he saw Sancho sitting at one of the desks. He was the man with the high-crowned hat. In the glow of his cigarette, Scott saw thin crafty features. The man was not looking in his direction.

Scott drew his machine pistol. The yellow barrel was already in position. He rose slowly to his feet, but some slight sound betrayed him.

"Caramba!" the man exclaimed, coming to his feet. "Who is there?"

Scott heard the whisper of a gun being slid from its holster. He fired his own pistol, twice in rapid succession. There was a faint hiss and with a choking gasp, Sancho staggered back and sank to the floor.

Scott went to the man, and examined him in the pencil beam of his torch. The miniature knock-out darts had struck Sancho in the left upper arm. The drug they contained had worked quickly. The man was probably unconscious before he hit the floor. Scott knew he would be out for an hour.

He made for the door to the left of the dais and eased it open. The room beyond was in darkness. No sound came from within.

Scott opened the door wider and cat-footed in, then probed the darkness with his pencil beam.

The room was small, with oak panelling, a beam ceiling and a stone fireplace. Where the hearth should have been yawned a hole.

Scott moved stealthily across the room. Below the hearth a stone stairway led down, but it was a stairway much older than the one he had seen in the professor's hacienda. This, he knew, had been in existence when Pizarro rode triumphantly into Cuzco. Down below, Inca treasures had probably been hidden from the conqueror.

A light came from beneath him. Faint voices drifted to his ears. Scott switched off his torch and slowly descended. There was a stone landing halfway down.

Scott crouched there, looking about him. The vault had stone grey walls. The upper parts were of the same massive blue-grey stone blocks that formed the old walls of the city. The lower parts were chiselled from bedrock. Firewood, barrels, lumber, old desks, and schoolbooks littered the place. Obviously it had been used as a storage cellar for years.

At the far end were the other three men. While one held a lamp, the others were levering with a crowbar at one of the stone blocks. Suddenly one of them cried out to the man with the lamp.

"It moves, Señor Morales! It moves!"

Scott watched fascinated as the heavy stone pivoted slowly to reveal a dark cavity.

Morales, a hard-faced man with a thin moustache, better

dressed than the others, shone the lamp into the hole, then thrust his hand inside and drew something out that gleamed in the lamplight.

It looked like a small gold casket. The men gasped at the sight of it.

Scott shared their excitement. That casket had lain there for six centuries. If the *quipu* did not lie, it might hold the key to untold wealth.

Scott saw that sweat was glistening on the olive-skinned face of the man called Morales as he fumbled with the fastening. Greed was etched on the swarthy faces of his companions as they watched.

Morales seemed to find difficulty in opening the casket, so cunningly had the ancient craftsman made it. With an angry snarl, he drew a knife and viciously attacked the delicate casket, which Scott figured was worth a minor fortune in itself. At last it burst open.

Morales snatched something from inside and held it up. Green fire flashed from his fingers.

"*Sacramento!*" gasped one of the men. "Never have I seen an emerald like that, Señor Morales."

"It would not amount to much between the six of us," Morales said impatiently. "We did not come all this way just to get a single emerald. There must be some other

reason for it being hidden here - wait!"

He shone his torch on the emerald. Scott saw that one surface was flat, as if it had been cut.

"Look," Morales said, excitement edging his voice. "Something is engraved on it. It looks like a plan or a map. Amigos, I believe it shows the location of the lost emerald mines of the Incas. Let us go."

Scott turned and crept up the stairs again. He didn't want to get caught. It would have been simple enough to have disposed of all three men with his knock-out darts, but unconscious men were of no use to him. He wanted them to lead him to where Lady Penelope and her cousin were being held.

He reached the small room above the vault and hurried through the darkness to the door leading into the hall, which he had left open.

As he stepped through a torch flashed in his eyes, blinding him. Something hard crashed down on his head which seemed to explode into a million light-shot fragments. Then he whirled down into black oblivion.

CHAPTER NINE

CRASH LANDING

Scott opened his eyes and stared dazedly at a dark stone wall a few inches from his face. At first, he thought he was back in the vault below the schoolhouse.

His head was sore and throbbing. He tried to raise his hand to it but found that he was handcuffed.

Scott struggled into a sitting position and looked about him. The dark stone wall was the wall of a cell. He was seated on a wooden bunk covered with a straw mattress. Above him was a barred window through which he could see the starry sky. Opposite the window was a gate of iron bars beyond which was a cold-looking stone corridor leading to other cells.

Keys jangled and footsteps came along the corridor. A burly woman in a white uniform and peaked cap appeared and looked through the bars at him.

"So," she said quietly in Spanish. "You have come round at last? Come, Americano! El Commandante wishes to see you."

She opened the gate and Scott rose unsteadily to his feet. For a moment the cell swam about him. Then he took a grip on himself and walked out into the corridor. He saw that the jailer was watching him warily and that she kept her hand near the butt of a pistol at her hip.

"What happened to me?" he asked.

The woman gestured along the corridor. "El Commandante is waiting."

Scott went down the corridor and into a bare lime-washed office where a grey-haired man in gold-braided uniform sat behind a desk. Against a wall a burly dark-skinned man in the clothes of a workman sat with his right arm in a sling. He stared stolidly at Scott.

Scott turned to the officer behind the desk, and then froze. On the desk were his machine pistol, his microradio transmitter and torch.

"What's the idea of the bracelets, commandant?" he asked, holding up his wrists.

"You are under arrest, señor. Unfortunately, your gang made good their escape."

"My gang?"

"With whom you broke into the school." The commandant indicated the man with his arm in a sling. "Señor Carmello, the janitor, remembered he had forgotten to lock the door and returned to the school. He found you there and struck you down, but one of your gang shot him and they got away."

"Now, look here, commandant," Scott said patiently. "You've got hold of the wrong end of the stick. I can explain."

"Explain these, if you please, Americano." The officer tapped the machine pistol and the radio. "I think you are a spy."

"That's ridiculous. I'm a member of International Rescue."

"So?" The other man laughed scornfully. "And I am the President of the United States."

Scott thought of Morales and his men getting farther away every moment, possibly taking Lady Penelope and her cousin with them.

"Let me use that radio and I'll contact someone who'll vouch for me, commandant."

"So you can send a message to your headquarters? I am not a fool, señor. You will go before the examining magistrate in the morning." He signed to the jailer. "Take him away."

Scott was thrust back down the corridor into the cell and the door clanged behind him.

He lay down on the bunk again. He realised there was nothing he could do, and his head was aching badly. His only hope was that Parker and the professor would arrive soon and convince the commandant that he was not a major threat to Peru's security.

Scott must have dozed off, because the next thing he knew keys were jangling in the corridor again, and dawn was turning to grey the square of sky framed in the window opening.

The jailer unlocked the gate and motioned him to come out. Scott rose wearily to his feet, and went down the corridor into the office. Relief surged through him when he saw Professor de Sabata talking agitatedly to the commandant.

The professor broke off what he was saying and turned to seize Scott's manacled hands.

"A thousand apologies, my friend! I am horrified that a countryman of mine should be so foolish as to think you are a dangerous criminal." He glanced at the commandant. "Please have these things removed from his wrists."

"At once, Señor Professor!"

At a sign from the commandant, the jailer unlocked the

handcuffs. It was evident that the professor's influence carried considerable weight in Cuzco.

"And now, my friend," the professor went on, "let us hear your side of the story."

Scott told him what had happened in the schoolhouse, and the professor's dark eyes gleamed.

"An emerald?" he mused. "And their leader said there was a plan engraved on it? What did he look like, this man?"

Scott described Morales.

"Morales? Caramba! I know him. An unscrupulous adventurer, my friend. A clever scoundrel who always manages to keep on the right side of the law. But he will stop at little if there is enough profit to be gained. I think it was lucky the janitor struck you down before they caught you."

He turned to the commandant. "Have the town searched for these men. Perhaps they are still here. Stop and search all trucks leaving the city."

"Si, Señor Professor."

As if eager to please, the commandant switched on an intercom microphone and spoke rapidly into it.

"I think it's a waste of time, professor," Scott said. "My guess is they've already left the city. Question is, which way have they gone?" He smiled bitterly. "If all roads lead to Cuzco as they say, I guess all roads lead out of it. They might have gone to any point of the compass."

"No, I think not," the professor said with a thoughtful frown. He took Scott's arm. "Come, we cannot talk freely in here."

Leaving the commandant still snapping orders into the intercom, they left the police station. Outside in the dawn light Parker was still dozing over the wheel of the Rolls. He woke up with a start as the professor tapped on the canopy, and the craggy face lit up at sight of Scott.

"Thank 'eavens you're orl right, guv." he said. "Sorry we couldn't make it quicker than wot we did, but them roads was carved up something awful in places by the earthquake. And when we did get 'ere we 'ad to chase round before we could find out what 'appened to you."

"That's okay," Scott grinned as he sank into the luxury of the back seat. "Guess things could have been worse." He turned to the professor who had got in beside him. "What's on your mind? You think you know which direction Morales and his gang may have taken?"

"Si, señor. I was telling you earlier of the priest of Pizarro who tortured the Incas trying to find out where the emerald mines were. Although he never discovered their exact location, he did extort a few clues from his unfortunate victims. One of them was that the mines were in the deep jungle to the east."

"So that's where you figure Morales will head?"

"Si, señor."

Scott's face tightened. "Well, that narrows it down considerably."

"Lumme, you're an optimist, Mister Scott," Parker put in. "There might be 'arf a dozen roads leading east from 'ere."

"You're forgetting Thunderbird One. Now it's getting light I can reconnoitre the whole of this territory from Ecuador to Bolivia in an hour. I guess not much traffic heads for the jungle, does it, professor?"

"Indeed not, my friend. Most of it is still as impenetrable as it was two centuries ago and many of the tribes are just as savage."

"Okay," said Scott. "I left Thunderbird One in a quarry to the north east. Let's get out there, Parker. I've got to locate those crooks before they reach the jungle. Once they do it'll be impossible to see them from the air."

As Thunderbird One rose vertically from the gloom of the quarry, the sun burst above the horizon with the sudden intensity of a nuclear explosion, flooding the bleak mountains with golden light.

It was easy to understand, Scott thought, why the ancient Incas had worshipped the sun, when their god rose in such a blaze of glory each morning.

Below him the mountains reared and folded like the waves of a storm-swept sea frozen to immobility.

As he hurtled north, arid plateaux devoid of life and deep canyons dark with vegetation flashed beneath him or streamed across the screens of his scanners. The only signs of life he saw were an occasional village of primitive Indian huts and a llama caravan making its slow way along a trail towards distant Cuzco.

He saw a section of an Inca road winding across a sheer mountain slope, its course still plainly visible from the air after centuries.

But modern roads were few, standing out like thin ribbons against the darkness of the terrain.

To the east, mountains dropped away, streams sparkled and cascaded down the slopes to form rivers that rushed towards the vast dark green ocean of the jungle stretching away into Amazonia, still untamed after centuries of exploration.

And still there was no sign of the truck he was seeking. It occurred to him that Morales might have abandoned the truck and taken to a plane, but he thought that unlikely. If the crook was aiming to penetrate that sea of jungle a truck would be a better bet than a plane, which would need landing fields and could not follow overgrown trails.

But Scott had a hunch it was no ordinary transport truck he was looking for. The odds were it was multipurpose, the kind that an expedition would use in treacherous terrain, with caterpillar tracks to supplement its road wheels or maybe even amphibious.

If Morales was the kind of man the professor had described, he would have left little to chance in his ruthless quest for the vast fortune that legend said was hidden somewhere in the ageless jungle.

Half an hour later he was up near the Ecuador border, but he had seen no sign of his quarry. Reason told him they could not have got so far in the time that had elapsed since he'd seen Morales and his men in the school at Cuzco.

He swung round and sent Thunderbird One screaming back over the lower slopes of the mountains just above the jungle line.

Scott switched on the radio and contacted the Rolls, which was somewhere to the south of him, heading east over the main road from Cuzco to the jungle on the assumption that Morales would have taken that route.

"No luck yet, Mister Scott?" asked Parker.

"No. But I reckon they haven't had time to reach the jungle yet. The odds are they can travel across country in that truck. I'll drop lower and scan some of these canyons. Can you cut across country if I locate them?"

"You bet," Parker said. "The Rolls can do anything except climb a precipice, Mister Scott."

"Swell. I'll maintain open circuit."

He screamed on southwards. Far ahead he saw the ribbon of the main east road appear, dipping into valleys and soaring over stony ridges until finally it flung itself across a trestle bridge over a chasm and vanished into the jungle.

To the west a deep canyon appeared, like a dark gash as if slashed in the mountain slope by a cosmic sword.

Scott reduced speed and extended his wings, planing down to scan the shadowy depths of the canyon.

And then he saw it.

Crawling on caterpillar tracks along the rock-strewn floor of the canyon was a closed truck, looking from that height like a great green bug.

Scott swooped low, his auto-cameras scanning, then swung in a big arc and came back over the canyon.

Briefly, he considered using the craft's powerful demolition cannon to create a rock fall, blocking the canyon to delay the truck and give Parker a chance of catching up with it. Then he thought better of it. There was no telling how Morales would react and what would become of Lady Penelope and her cousin if he were to take such an action.

His jaw tightened when he saw a small hatch slide back at the front of the streamlined canopy of the truck, and the nozzle of a gun appeared. Accelerating, he flung Thunderbird One upwards.

On his scanner screen he got a glimpse of the gun flashing. There was no time to retract his wings. He brought Thunderbird One round in a loop, corkscrewed and levelled out two thousand yards away from the canyon.

"They sure mean business," he gasped. "If my reaction had been a split second slower—"

A red light flashed. An urgent bleeping sounded from the control panel.

Homing missile!

The thought had scarcely registered when something exploded at the tail of the craft. It shuddered and bucked violently. But for the straps Scott would have been flung from his seat.

Lights were winking on the control panel. A quick glance told him he was in dire trouble. The jets were not firing. Thunderbird One was rapidly losing height. He thanked his stars he had not had time to retract the wings or already she would be plummeting earthwards like a meteor to obliterate herself against the rocky terrain.

Even so, the rarefied air was not holding her as it would have done at a lower altitude. The mountain slope seemed to be rushing up to meet him.

Desperately he jigged the manual controls, trying to gain height.

He felt a little lift, but that mountainside was perilously near.

Far ahead he could see the ribbon of the main road along which the Rolls was travelling. Could he reach it before he crash-landed? He doubted it.

An air current, sweeping off the mountain, suddenly lifted the diving craft, giving him hope. He found the machine answering reluctantly to the steering controls.

Scott banked away from the mountain. Ahead he saw a small valley open up, dark with jungle. He realised it might be his only hope. If he landed among the cushioning trees, he might have a chance of saving Thunderbird One. If he hit the rocky terrain the aircraft would be shattered and what little was left would probably be blown to atoms by its exploding fuel tanks.

It was typical of Scott, as of all his brothers, that not once did he think of ejecting himself and parachuting down to safety. Thunderbird One had to be saved from destruction if it were humanly possible.

A few seconds later he knew he was going to make it. The air current had been his salvation, buoying him up. Over the valley he could see warm air rising from the steaming jungle.

It tended to take him up with it. But to overshoot the valley would be fatal. Deliberately he nose-dived.

Gritting his teeth, Scott prepared for the shock. He tried not to think what would happen if the matted green mass could not withstand the weight of the aircraft.

At the last moment he brought the nose up and skimmed feet above the tops of the trees, then pancaked, plunging into that green sea at the shallowest of angles.

He heard great boughs snap against the hull. Then the sky was blotted out and through the observation window there was just a blur of green.

Slower…slower…but was it slow enough?

And then thick lianas, vines as thick as his wrists took hold like the hawsers on the flight deck of an aircraft carrier, braking the plunging craft, parting reluctantly beneath its great weight, and then, with incredible gentleness, allowing it to slide between two massive twisted trunks of mahogany to bury its nose deep in the soft dank earth beneath.

Scott cuffed the sweat from his brow, and tried the radio. But he could get no response from it. The monitor screen was dead too. He tried the short-range micro-transmitter and presently contacted Parker.

"I've been trying to get you, Mister Scott," he said anxiously. "Wot 'appened?"

Scott told him. "Can you get a fix on me?"

Parker was silent for a few moments, then said, "You're roughly fifty miles north-north-east of us, Mister Scott."

"Okay, start making tracks towards me. Radio base and report what's happened. Give them the approximate position of this valley. Virgil will be able to locate Thunderbird One easily enough with his scanners even if she's not visible from the air."

"Wot about you, guv?"

"I'll start walking towards you."

"Lumme! Through that jungle? With all them 'orrid snakes an' Annie Condas an' things? You got more guts than I 'ave."

Scott smiled. He couldn't imagine Parker being scared of much.

"I'll be okay, Parker," he said. "Guess my machine pistol can take care of anything I'm likely to run up against. You might have trouble forcing your way through the jungle anyway, and every hour we can save may be vital. Morales probably reckons he's safe from pursuit now he's shot me down. Be seeing you. I'll maintain radio contact to give you a bearing."

"Okey doke, sir. Good luck!"

Scott remembered the scanner films he'd been taking of the truck before he was shot down.

One of the cameras had an X-ray lens. He took out the film and ran it through a mercury battery-operated projector.

A clear picture of the interior of the truck came on the screen. He could identify Morales and Sancho, the man he had knocked out with his pistol in the schoolroom at Cuzco. Sancho was driving.

At the rear of the truck, he could just make out the trussed figures of Lady Penelope and the young man he had seen carried from the ruins of the restaurant in Lima.

"That settles one thing," he muttered. "We're not on a wild goose chase."

Scott put overalls on over his uniform. They would make it warm going through the jungle, but he didn't take lightly Parker's word about snakes.

Anacondas, if he encountered any, would be easily dealt with by the machine pistol, but smaller, venomous snakes, that might lie unseen beside his path to dart their deadly lightning fangs at him, were another matter. The tough overalls would give him protection against them.

Scott made up a pack of emergency rations. Then arming himself with a small hatchet, hacking knife, a laser beam and his machine pistol, he opened the hatch, closed it behind him and slid down a vine to the ground.

For a moment or so he stood there, listening to the noises

of the jungle all around him. Something slithered through the rank grass. From a distance came the squealing of some small animal in deadly peril. A tiny bird with rainbow plumage flew twittering, close enough to his head to make him duck. A parakeet squawked.

Scott took one last look at the wrecked plane towering above him. No further harm could come to it here. And in an hour or so Thunderbird Two would be zooming down and Virgil would take over.

Scott took a compass bearing, then resolutely plunged south-south-west into the fetid jungle.

Presently he struck a swift-running stream, tumbling down from the mountains. He stopped to drink and bathe his sweating face. The water was icy cold.

Then he went on again, following the course of the stream.

In the lounge of the tropical island house, Jeff Tracy looked grimly at Virgil.

"I sure hope Scott's not biting off more than he can chew in going after those scoundrels with just Parker to back him."

Virgil smiled. "They're a pretty tough twosome, Dad. Besides they've got no choice if Lady Penelope and her cousin are to be saved. Who knows what those crooks might do with them if they should find that emerald mine!"

"Guess you're right, son. Maybe you can get out there soon enough to give a hand, anyway. Get going. You'll need Brains and his workshop pod. Better take Gordon along, too."

"Okay. I'm on my way, Dad!" Virgil said eagerly, quickly crossing the room to put his back against the picture panel of the rocket craft.

Some minutes later, Jeff stood at the window overlooking the pool, watching the huge green jet plane thundering off its launch ramp into a cloudless blue Pacific sky.

There was a little tightness in his throat, and apprehension mingled with the pride that swelled his heart.

"Half our outfit's tied up out there in that godforsaken country," he murmured. "If those boys shouldn't come back..."

CHAPTER TEN

GUARDIANS OF THE GREEN FLAME

"Where to now, sir?" Parker asked nearly an hour later when he picked up Scott in the Rolls on the arid stony plateau above the valley.

"Head east. We've got to find that canyon where I saw the truck, and trail it."

Scott broke off, glancing up at the sky.

"Wot's the matter, guv?"

Scott indicated a tiny black shape high up against the cloudless blue sky.

"A condor," the professor suggested. "It's been following us for quite a while now."

"That's no condor," Scott said thoughtfully. "Got some glasses, Parker?"

Parker handed him a powerful pair of binoculars and Scott focused on the black object. His lips tightened.

"It's a 'copter. Looks like the heli-jet that guy Hood escaped in at the professor's place last night."

"So he's been trailin' us, huh?"

"I suspect he was trailing you all night, Parker."

Almost as if the pilot had become aware they were discussing him, the heli-jet hurtled away towards the distant jungle.

"We've got our hands full with Morales and his gang without having to worry about that joker," Scott said. "Get cracking, Parker."

The big car hurtled eastwards down the long gentle slope of the plateau at a speed that put even Scott's heart in his mouth.

The professor, clinging grimly to a strap, smiled weakly at him. "Mad," he murmured. "Quite mad, like all the English."

Twenty minutes and as many detours later they reached the bottom of the canyon, but Scott estimated they had not travelled more than ten miles east, and his hopes of overtaking Morales' truck before it lost itself in the jungle were fading rapidly.

On the canyon floor, however, they made rapid progress, following the tracks of the truck beside a mountain stream. In places where the canyon had been choked by undergrowth a path had been scorched, and the dry brush, back against the canyon walls, was still smouldering.

"Must be using a flame thrower," Scott said. "Morales sure came prepared for every trick."

They crossed a swift-flowing river on the hydrofoils, and entered another canyon.

The radio bleeped and Virgil's voice came through.

"Scott from Thunderbird Two. Can you read me?"

Taking the microphone from Parker, Scott said, "Come in, Virgil. Where are you?"

"We've located Thunderbird One. Brains is inspecting the damage. He figures it may be quite a long job to repair. What's the set-up?"

Scott told him.

"Would you like me to make an air reconnaissance to see if I can locate that truck?" asked Virgil.

Scott considered, then said, "No, thanks, Virgil. We'll be into the jungle pretty soon and I guess you'd have a tough task of spotting it. Besides, if Morales saw you he'd know International Rescue was still on his tail. That might not be so good for Lady Penelope. And he might try to shoot you down as he did me. Guess we'll carry on as we are."

"Can the Rolls make it through the jungle? How about my returning to base to get the jungle cat?"

Scott thought of the amphibious caterpillar crawler that could claw and blast its way through the dense jungle. The idea was tempting, but...

"It would take all of three or four hours for you to get it back here from base, Virgil," he said. "Anything might happen in that time. I've got to stick as close to Morales as I can. I've got a hunch he won't find the jungle much of an obstacle. If he blazes a trail for the truck, I guess the Rolls can get through the same way."

When at last they reached the jungle, after following the remnants of an old Inca road for some miles, Scott found that his hunch was right.

For a swath had been cut through the thick-growing forest as if by a powerful heat ray, forming a tunnel with

seared and blackened walls from which the acrid odour of burning mingled with the fetid stench of decaying vegetation.

They followed the burned trail for hours. Water was no obstacle. Once the amphibious truck ahead had taken to a wide river, travelling downstream for some miles. Relentlessly they followed, the whine of the aquajet power-pack on the rear hydrofoil mingling with the swish of water and the cries and screechings from the teeming jungle that flanked them.

Back again into the jungle they went. Jaguars snarled at them and fled. Huge boas, as thick as a man's thigh, writhed away, yellow eyes gleaming hate.

About mid-afternoon they halted in a small clearing.

They had covered nearly two hundred miles since first entering the jungle and as yet they had seen no sign of human habitation.

While Parker set up the paratrooper stove to make coffee, Scott and the professor stretched their legs.

"Any idea how much further we may have to go, Professor?" Scott asked anxiously. "It's only about three hours to sundown."

The professor shrugged his slim shoulders. "It is impossible to say, señor. Only Morales knows where he is going. For centuries men have searched for the legendary emerald mines. They would have been found long since if they were easy to—"

The words froze on his lips as a long wooden spear whistled out of the jungle to pluck his broad-brimmed hat from his head before quivering in the earth beside the Rolls. Parker spun round with a startled gasp, upsetting the stove.

Scott clawed out his machine pistol and swung in the direction from which the spear had come.

He saw a dark face among the foliage, contorted with hate, saw the gleam of the point of another upraised spear. He fired. The tiny paralysing dart sped for its target even as the spear came hissing towards him. Scott ducked and saw the man who had thrown it topple forward into the clearing, unconscious.

The tribesman was naked except for a cloth about his waist. He had straight black hair and dark skin, and there were round wooden lugs thrust through the pierced lobes of his ears. His toes were curiously splayed, with the big toe separated from the rest. On each cheek and on his chest a red triangle was painted.

Indifferent to danger, the professor stared fascinated at the unconscious man. Scott grabbed his arm and thrust him towards the car.

"Quick!" he said. "Get under cover. There may be others about."

They scrambled inside, and Scott grunted with relief when the bullet proof canopy closed tightly around them.

"Get her moving, Parker," he ordered.

As the Rolls lurched forwards onto the path that Morales' truck had seared through the jungle, Scott turned to the professor, whose dark eyes were gleaming with excitement.

"You seem mighty interested in that guy who tried to skewer you, professor. I didn't think tribes so primitive still existed."

"My friend, did you see those triangles painted on him?" the professor asked eagerly.

"Sure."

"That is the sign of the Incas. The triangle has always been identified with their buildings. Their thatched roofs were that shape, and their windows."

"You mean that fellow was an Inca?" Scott said incredulously. "You mean *that*'s what the descendants of the men who built those marvellous roads and fortresses and temples and shifted all those huge blocks of stone, have become after all this time?"

"No, my friend. I believe that man was one of the fabled Guardians of the Green Flame."

"What green flame?"

"*Emeralds!* If my theory is right, señor, that man is one of a tribe with whom legend says the Inca emperor Tupac Yupanquy made a blood pact hundreds of years ago."

"Go on," Scott said, his pulses quickening now. "What's the rest of the story, professor?"

"It is said that the legendary emerald mines were discovered in Tupac's reign and to protect them he made a royal decree, designating a savage tribe of jungle tribesmen as 'guardians of the green flame'. He demanded a blood oath from them, binding them to attack and kill all strangers who entered their territory, with the exception of members of the royal family of the Incas of course."

"That's why the emerald mines were never discovered?"

"Possibly. It has always been known that there was a primitive tribe deep in the jungle who hate everyone outside their own tribe and kill without mercy. Very few outsiders have seen them and returned to speak of them. They seldom show themselves, but instead attack from cover with their lances and arrows, which are probably tipped with poison. Those of other tribes say the witchdoctors of these mysterious savages carry a green eye. It is their insignia of office and the source of their magic."

"That green eye is an emerald, huh?"

"That is what I believe, my friend."

"And you think this tribe is still guarding the emerald mines?"

"Why not?"

"But the Incas have been gone for six hundred years, Professor. How could they make a blood oath stick all this time?"

The professor smiled. "Remember these are very primitive savages, my friend, their lives bound by taboos. The legend also relates that the Incas erected a small temple near the site of the mines and placed in it a gold statue of Illa Tica, their goddess of creation. Around it they wove superstitions that so terrified the tribe that none of them would violate the taboo for fear of dying horribly."

Scott stared out at the blackened edge of the jungle tunnel streaming past the speeding Rolls.

It was an incredible story, but deep down he knew it could be true. Morales and his gang must believe it or they would not be burning their way feverishly through the jungle ahead of them.

They reached another river running north-east, a tributary of the mighty Amazon itself, the professor thought. Their trail followed it for some miles, then crossed it. Alligators raised ugly snouts above the murky water as the Rolls skimmed across on its hydrofoils.

A few miles downstream on the other side a smaller river joined it. Their trail turned east up this.

It was getting dark now and Scott realised he would be faced with a problem, whether to halt for the night or press on in the light of the car's powerful headbeams. Urgency was essential, but so was security.

He did not know how far ahead Morales was. But suppose *he* stopped for the night? He would be warned of their approach by the powerful headlights. Knowing the weapons with which the truck was armed, Scott realised the Rolls would not stand a chance even with the powerful cannon which was concealed behind the radiator.

As the darkness closed in, Parker said, "Wot's that light through the trees, Mister Scott? Looks like a fire."

Scott told him to stop, and peered at the red glow in the gloom some distance ahead.

Had his hunch been right? Had Morales stopped for the night? But why light a fire when his truck must be a fully equipped camp on wheels?

There was obviously only one way to find out. He checked his pistol and his laser beam, put his micro-radio in his pocket, and inserted a tiny speaker plug in his ear.

"Okay, Parker," he said. "Open up. I'll reconnoitre."

Parker gasped. "Lumme, guv! You ain't goin' out there among all them wotsits?"

"I'm well-armed."

"But you ain't got eyes in your back. I'm comin' with you."

"You'll stay here and—well, if anything does happen to me, it's up to you and the professor to get to Lady Penelope. Remember, your first duty's to her, Parker. If I need help, I'll radio."

Grumbling, Parker acquiesced and opened the canopy. Scott got out, flipped his hand and moved ahead into the darkness.

As he drew nearer, he saw that the fire glow was coming from some distance to the right of the path Morales' truck had seared. Warily he pushed through the jungle towards it, his machine pistol held ready, alert for the slightest sign of danger. Trailing vines brushed his face and snagged his booted feet. Huge white orchids glowed like pale ghostly faces in the fetid gloom.

Presently the pungent smell of wood smoke touched his nostrils and then, as the matted undergrowth cleared a little, he saw the palm-thatched huts of a tribal village in the fire glow.

He heard a weird flute-like sound, and then a sudden high-pitched scream stopped him in his tracks, chilling the blood in his veins.

"You orl right, Mister Scott?" asked Parker's hoarse voice in his ear.

"Yes."

"Wot was that scream?"

"It came from a tribal village."

Another blood-curdling screech echoed through the jungle and then other voices were screeching in a strange off-beat cadence, keeping time to the weird pipings.

"Stand by, Parker!" he said. "Something's happening in the village. I'm going to take a look."

He moved forward slowly, carefully parting the undergrowth and peering out into the clearing where the village stood.

There were six huts, raised a few feet from the ground on poles, crude structures with an open platform on two sides of a communal room with a screen door of bamboo.

In the centre of the clearing was a fire and round it squatted some fifty villagers, men, women and children. All the men were daubed with red triangles like those Scott had seen on the one who had tried to spear the professor.

They were swaying and screeching in time to a bamboo flute which one of them was playing, and their eyes were fixed on a grotesque figure who sat with his back to one of the huts.

He had a headdress of red feathers and in one hand he held by its long black hair a shrunken human head, no bigger than a doll's. He seemed to be crooning to it.

Round his neck a huge emerald was suspended, which seemed alive with green flames in the light of the fire.

Suddenly the witch doctor uttered a piercing shriek and

leapt to his feet, dancing wildly, shaking and shivering as if in a fit, and waving the gruesome head. White froth appeared about his hideous mouth.

Then he leapt up the crude ladder that led to the hut and flung aside the bamboo screen.

Scott's mouth went dry.

Sitting bound to a chair made in the crude semblance of a throne, was Lady Penelope, her hair gleaming like gold in the glow of the fire, her lovely blue eyes wide with terror.

CHAPTER ELEVEN

GODDESS OF CREATION

Scott raised his pistol, covering the witch doctor, then relaxed a little as the savage leapt down again to the ground and resumed his dance, jerking and swaying and uttering piercing shrieks.

The other men rose from the fire and joined him, prancing round, howling and screeching and waving their arms wildly. At every gyration they bowed to the still figure which sat up in the entrance to the hut, almost as if worshipping her, Scott thought.

For the moment she seemed in no danger. But what happened when that fiendish dance was over?

Parker's voice sounded in his ear plug. "For Pete's sake wot goes on, guv?"

"Lady Penelope's here, a prisoner of the natives. I'm getting her away. Stand by, Parker!"

"Righto, guv. But if they…"

His gruff voice trailed off, but Scott knew how he felt.

"Quit worrying, Parker. Just be ready to move off when we get to you."

Scott snapped the yellow barrel of his pistol into position and took deliberate aim, pumping three miniature knockout darts at the leaping, screaming witch doctor.

The darts struck him in the shoulder while he was

in mid-air. He landed on his feet, tried to spring again, staggered, then fell headlong and lay still.

The other natives stopped dancing, staring down in wonder at him. The women and children cowered away, hiding their faces behind their hands.

A deathly stillness fell on the clearing, broken only by the hissing of wood on the fire.

Scott took advantage of their terror to change the yellow barrel of his pistol for a blue one. Then he fired a succession of shots into the ground about the fire. Dense blue-grey fumes billowed up to mingle with the fire smoke as the tiny shells exploded, drifting across the clearing like a fog.

Coming so soon after the mysterious striking down of their witch doctor, it was too much for the tribespeople. They fled screaming into their huts.

Drawing his knife, Scott raced through the fog across the clearing and swarmed up the rickety ladder to the witch doctor's hut.

Lady Penelope gasped with relief when she recognised him.

"Scott! Thank goodness!"

"Save your breath," he panted, cutting the liana ropes that bound her. "You'll need it to get back through that smoke screen."

When she was free she rose eagerly to her feet, then gave a little cry and would have toppled from the platform if Scott hadn't caught her.

"Awfully sorry, dear boy," she murmured. "Pins and needles, you know. Silly of me, but—"

Scott swept her off her feet and slung her over his shoulder. At any moment some of the locals might recover from their terror and creep out again to investigate. He leapt from the platform and raced back across the clearing, crashing through the undergrowth, expecting at every step to feel the searing impact of a spear in his back.

At last he was through to the track and saw the faintly gleaming shape of the Rolls a few yards away.

Parker had the canopy open. Scott bundled Lady Penelope

unceremoniously into the rear seat beside the professor and clambered in after her.

"Get going, Parker," he gasped.

The gull-wing doors closed and the big car leapt forward down the track, its headlights blazing. In their beam Scott caught a glimpse of a bunch of tribespeople charging through the undergrowth, spears brandished. One spear rattled futilely on the canopy and then the Rolls went hurtling past.

"Really, Scott," Lady Penelope smiled, rubbing her chafed wrists. "You're wasted with International Rescue. You should be on the telefilms. You'd be simply terrific as a twenty-first century Tarzan."

"Thanks, but I guess I'll stick to the rescue business," Scott chuckled. "Less strain on the nervous system. But how did you get into that village?"

Her blue eyes hardened. "Charming Señor Morales bartered me."

"Bartered you? For what?"

"For a guide and a safe passage to the temple of Illa Tica, whatever that is."

"The Inca goddess of creation," the professor said. "According to the legend she guards the gateway to the emerald mines. No Indian will go past her temple."

"But Morales will," Scott said. "How far is he ahead of us, Lady Penelope?"

"About an hour."

"Does he know we're trailing him?"

"If he did, he would have done something about it. He thinks he shot you down."

"He did," Scott said grimly. "But we Tracys have a habit of bouncing back. He's still got your cousin, of course?"

"Yes. Gus has recovered his memory. I thought at first Morales wanted him because he knew more about the emerald mines than the *quipu* revealed, but since getting that emerald in Cuzco I think Morales is keeping him as a hostage."

"Against what?"

"If he finds the mines he's still got to get away with the loot."

"You mean he doesn't trust those natives?"

Lady Penelope smiled. "You saw them. Would you?"

"Shall I keep the 'eadlights on, Mister Scott?" Parker asked. "They rather h'advertise our presence to the h'enemy."

"Can you drive on your sidelights?"

"Yes, sir. And the h'instruments will pick up the h'enemy before we get in sight."

"Okay."

Scott turned to Lady Penelope. "Just what were those people aiming to do to you? It looked as though they were worshipping you."

"I gathered they regarded me as some kind of a - er - goddess."

"It is possible," said the professor. "Fair-haired people were regarded as gods by many of the ancient races of South America. They believed they were true children of the sun because of the colour of their hair. There are legends of a golden-haired race who once ruled the continent, long before the Incas, and who promised to return to save the people when they were in dire need."

Lady Penelope frowned. "I suspect that Señor Morales had something like that in mind when he left Cuzco. Some of his men wanted to - er - dispose of Gus and I. To shut our mouths, as they rather crudely put it. Señor Morales over-ruled them, to my great relief."

"Why should Morales be scared of a little bunch of natives like that lot back there?" Scott asked. "With his weapons he could wipe them out."

"But that is not all of the tribe, my friend," put in Professor de Sabata. "There are many villages scattered throughout this jungle territory. A message on the drums would bring the whole tribe down on Señor Morales. That might not be so healthy for him. He is no fool. He thinks it better to buy their friendship by giving them a goddess."

They drove on through the night. The trail was climbing now, leaving the swampier lower levels of the jungle and following a river valley into the hills. But the going became more difficult and at times they were making only a few miles an hour. Now and then sheer precipices yawned below them in the moonlight, and it would have been suicide to have attempted to travel faster.

At hourly intervals Scott reported progress to Virgil, who came through just before dawn to report that Brains had repaired Thunderbird One.

"Just say the word and we'll be with you in a few minutes, Scott. Gordon and I are bored stiff kicking our heels and holding tools for Brains."

"Hold on a bit longer," Scott told him. "Morales has still got Lady Penelope's cousin as hostage. If he sees you coming he might get nasty with him."

"We're beginning to figure you want to hog all the fun, big brother."

"Fun?" Scott smiled grimly and glanced from the window beside him. "Right now we're about a thousand feet up with twelve inches between our offside wheels and eternity."

"Don't exaggerate, dear boy," Lady Penelope murmured, "it is only ten inches."

As dawn began to tinge the sky above the eastern mountains, they were moving along the edge of a narrow plateau, following the trail the truck had blazed through thick scrub, when there came an insistent high-pitched bleeping from the dashboard.

"I believe the h'enemy is just ahead," Parker said quietly.

"Okay, stop," Scott said. "I'll reconnoitre."

"I'll come with you, Scott," Lady Penelope volunteered. "It is about time I stretched my legs."

Leaving the car, they made their way stealthily forward.

There was no sound but the muffled roaring of a river in the chasm below the plateau rim to their right.

Suddenly Scott checked. The ground under his feet seemed to tremble and there was a rumbling deep down in the earth. Lady Penelope gripped his arm.

"What was that, Scott?"

"Just another earth tremor. I was warned in Lima that they might go on for days yet. Nothing to worry about, I guess."

They went on again, and then, as they turned a bend in the path, they froze.

In the gloom of half dawn, not fifty yards ahead of them stood Morales' truck, without lights. There was no sign of life.

Scott switched on his micro-radio and extended a tiny bowl antenna, directing it at the truck. At that range the sensitive microphone would pick up low conversation, even the snores of sleeping men. But he heard only the roar of the river below.

"They must have gone ahead on foot," Scott whispered. "Strange they haven't posted a guard."

"They're near the loot and they don't trust one another," she murmured.

Warily they approached the truck. Then, from the undergrowth near the truck, where he had apparently been sleeping, a tribesman arose. He stared at them in the grey light of dawn, then grabbed a spear which was sticking in the ground.

Scott snatched out his pistol, but Lady Penelope was quicker.

With a lightning flick of her hand, she tossed something at the native. It burst on his bare chest with a little plop. He gasped and the half-raised spear fell from his nerveless hand. His legs buckled and he pitched forward on his face and lay still.

Scott looked at Lady Penelope. "What was that?"

"A knockout gas capsule disguised as a lipstick case. I find them very convenient in tight corners, Scott."

The truck was sealed, but an inspection through the

windows, in the light of their torches, satisfied them that Gus was not in it. Apparently, Morales had taken him on as well.

Moving along a path which had been hacked through the tall brush, in the faint dawn light they saw a small pyramidical temple of dark stone blocks erected in three tiers against the base of a high cliff. It was partly overgrown by brush and its upper half was lost in the gloom.

"The temple of Illa Tica," Lady Penelope murmured. "But where is the Goddess of Creation?"

Almost as if the words had invoked a magic spell, the sun suddenly burst above the mountains and its searching rays lit up a golden statue seated on a rocky throne on the uppermost tiers of the temple.

"Guess that's the lady," Scott said in a low voice, awed by the sudden transition.

For centuries now the rising sun must have shone down on that statue, sitting there and guarding the secret treasure of the Incas.

The path led into the overgrown entrance to the temple. As they walked forward warily, Scott found himself glancing involuntarily at the statue above him. Was it just fancy or did its gleaming face scowl disapprovingly at him?

He grinned tightly. The savages from whom he had rescued Lady Penelope might believe in such superstition, but a twenty-first century mind should be above such things. And yet...

A few stone steps rose up beyond the entrance. Mounting these they found themselves in a stone-paved courtyard overgrown with tall weeds and trailing vines and lit up by sunlight. Before them was another stone gateway, gloomy and forbidding.

"There's a touch of the Sleeping Beauty about this," Scott muttered.

"But the Beauty's up there on that throne instead of lying on a couch waiting for us to awaken her, Scott."

"Sure. And she's been sleeping for five hundred years, not a hundred. Come on!"

They entered the second gateway. Here the sun could not penetrate. Scott probed the darkness with his microradio bug before switching on his torch. In its light he saw a big bare stone-paved chamber. Even the weeds had not gained a foothold here.

The walls were of stone blocks, so finely cut they fitted exactly. It would have been impossible to insert the blade of a knife between them. At intervals niches had been left in the wall and in them stood small statues which gleamed in the light of the torch.

"Probably coated with gold leaf," Scott whispered. "But I guess they'd still be worth a small fortune."

At the far end of the temple chamber a high altar had been cut from the solid cliff rock.

On the altar sat another statue whose head was a model of the sun with a streamer of fire radiating from it.

"The Sun God," Scott whispered. "Guess that's solid gold."

"Scott!" Lady Penelope whispered eagerly, clutching his arm. "Look!"

He shone his torch where she was pointing, and saw that part of the base of the altar had been rolled away to reveal a dark cavity into which were stone steps leading downwards.

Lady Penelope looked up at him. "That must be the way Morales went. It must be the entrance to the emerald mines."

"Guess so." Scott hesitated. Eager though he was to follow, it would be foolhardy to take unnecessary risks. There were six ruthless men down below. "We'll go back for help."

"Why not radio for them?"

"Too risky. Morales might pick up the transmission. Besides, we'd need more equipment."

They hurried back to the car, and Scott got Parker to dismantle the laser beam gun which was installed in the rear of the vehicle. Not only was it a devastating weapon, but it could cut through a thick rock wall in a matter of minutes.

Scott looked at the professor, who was watching the preparation with interest.

"You can stay in the car if you'd rather, professor."

His bearded face lit up eagerly. "*Caramba!* Am I a piece of sugar, señor, that I will melt if exposed to danger? We are about to make the discovery of the century and you suggest I should stay behind. Do not fear. If it comes to it, señor, I can handle a gun."

"Okay."

Before leaving, Scott radioed Virgil and told him what they had discovered.

"Stand by. If you don't hear from us in half an hour, take off. You'll be able to home on the Rolls. I'm leaving a radio beacon working."

"F.A.B., Scott."

Scott led the way back to the temple. As they came in sight of it, there was another earth tremor, so violent this time that it threw them off their feet.

As they lay sprawling, the professor pointed to the statue above the temple.

"Look!" he gasped.

They stared up at the statue. It was rocking violently. Suddenly it toppled from the throne and crashed down onto the roof of the temple.

In the silence that followed they looked nervously at one another.

"*Sacramento!*" the professor murmured. "To think that it has sat there for centuries and now it falls."

"It's a h'omen, that's wot it is!" Parker said hoarsely.

"Don't be silly, Parker," Lady Penelope said, getting to her feet. "It's merely a coincidence. No doubt every earth tremor over the centuries has rocked that statue a little and this one was the - er - last straw that broke the camel's back. Is that not so, professor?"

"Si, señorita. It can be nothing else."

But Scott thought that, for a man of science, he did not sound so sure of himself.

"Of course, Parker," went on Lady Penelope, "if you are scared you can go back and wait in the car."

"'Oo said I was scared?" he demanded with dignity. "I was just h'expressin' an opinion. But the sooner we rescue the 'onourable Gus and get the perishin' blazes out of 'ere the better I'm goin' to like it, m'lady."

They moved on into the gloom of the temple, Scott in the lead and Parker bringing up the rear, carrying the laser gun.

A few minutes after they had vanished a tiny black shape, that had been hovering up in the sky over the cliff, swooped down like a vulture to land before the temple.

The Hood grinned evilly as he alighted from his heli-jet, and made for the entrance.

CHAPTER TWELVE

TRAPPED

"Looks like some kind of chamber ahead," Scott whispered.

For some minutes they had been walking cautiously along a passage hewn through the solid rock, following the footprints of Morales and his men in the dust of centuries.

Scott dipped his torch, probing the darkness ahead with his radio bug. There was a deep murmuring sound, like distant rushing water, he thought. But there was nothing to indicate that their quarry was close ahead.

Warily he went on, flashing his torch about him. He saw he was in a circular, domed chamber about a hundred feet across. It was too symmetrical to have been fashioned by nature. There was no one in it.

Mineral flecks sparkled in the rock, but there was no flash of green fire that would indicate the presence of emeralds.

"What's that, Scott?" asked Lady Penelope in a hushed voice, as something on the floor against the wall gleamed whitely in the torch light.

Scott moved closer, then icy needles seemed to probe his spine when he saw a skull leering at him from a heap of human bones.

"A - a skellyton!" Parker gasped.

"It's not the only one," Scott said, sweeping the torch beam along the base of the wall.

At intervals of a few feet there were other heaps of bones with hideously grinning skulls. Above them hung chains of bronze riveted to the wall, still secured to the limbs of the skeletons by bands of copper.

"Swipe me!" Parker said hoarsely. "They must 'ave been chained there till they conked out."

"No doubt the remains of slaves who worked the emerald mines for the Incas," the professor said. "They would have been forced to live underground so they could never reveal the secret of the mines."

"Poor blokes," Parker muttered. "Then they was just left to die of starvation?"

"When the Spaniards conquered Peru and the royal Incas were killed, these unfortunate men were probably just forgotten."

They counted thirty heaps of bones as they moved round the wall of the chamber.

Then they found another passage opening from the chamber. The footprints of Morales and his men led down it. The sound of rushing water was louder now.

Suddenly the rock floor of the passage dropped away beneath the beam of Scott's torch. He found himself looking down a hewn shaft, a few feet in diameter. Perhaps twenty feet below was the floor of another chamber. Fixed to the nearer wall of the shaft was a bronze ladder. The sound of the water was a soft roaring now.

"Sounds like a subterranean river," he told the others. "Guess it's the one that runs through the chasm below the plateau where the temple is. Wait here. I'll see what's down there."

Switching off his torch, so as not to make a target for anyone who might be below, Scott lowered himself into the darkness over the edge of the shaft. He tested the ladder rungs with his feet. They seemed as firm as they had been centuries before when they were forged. Slowly he descended. He counted twenty-five rungs before his feet touched solid rock again.

Scott stood there listening with his radio bug. He could

hear nothing but the roaring of the underground river. The air was now damp with its spray.

Putting his back against the foot of the ladder, Scott drew his machine pistol before switching on his torch. But the chamber exposed in the probing beam of light was deserted.

It was about forty feet across, bulging out from the shaft like a bulbous bottle from its neck. A few feet to his right boiled the river in a rock channel. It rushed from one tunnel in the rock wall and vanished into another leading in the direction from the upper passage.

The footprints they were following led beside the river to the opening of another passage at the far side of the chamber.

Scott flashed a signal up the shaft and presently the others joined him. They crossed the chamber and entered the passage. It angled sharply downwards and then levelled out. As the sound of the river faded, Scott was able to use the radio bug again. They had gone about a hundred yards from the river when the sensitive microphone picked up a strange staccato sound.

Scott motioned to the others to stop and switched off the torch. Far ahead a faint glow appeared.

"Wait here," he whispered, going on alone.

As the light became brighter, the staccato sound grew louder. Presently he could make out the exit to the passage. A brilliant light shone beyond.

A few moments later he was peering into another roughly circular rock chamber, illuminated by a powerful portable arc lamp. In its light six men, stripped to the waist, were working feverishly at the rock face. One of them was using a self-powered drill. That accounted for the staccato sound he'd heard.

The men were prising pieces of rock from the wall that flashed like green fire in the light of the arc lamp. He was able to identify Morales and Sancho. The others he could not see plainly.

For a few moments Scott stared, fascinated by the sight of this legend of fabulous riches come true.

Then he brought his mind back to reality. Where was Lady Penelope's cousin?

Pistol at the ready, he moved silently into the chamber, scanning the shadows for a bound figure. Suddenly he sensed a movement behind him.

He swung, saw a dim figure lunging at him and the faint gleam of an upraised weapon.

Scott leapt aside and something crashed down on his left shoulder, numbing it. Turning, he brought the barrel of his pistol hard against the skull of his assailant. With a choking cry the man collapsed at his feet.

But the sound of the brief struggle must have been heard. The stuttering of the drill stopped. Scott swung defensively, biting his lip against the pain that was now racing through his shoulder. The other men were looking towards him.

It was then that he saw that one of the men was Gus. Evidently Morales had forced Gus to work while the sixth member of the gang kept guard.

Morales leapt to the arc lamp and spun it on its stand. The powerful light beamed out at Scott, dazzling him.

"International Rescue!" Morales shouted, recognising his uniform.

Instinctively Scott flung himself to the ground. A gun blazed and an explosive bullet detonated against the rock wall above him.

The yellow barrel with its magazine of paralysing darts was still in Scott's pistol, but he dared not fire at the men for fear of hitting Gus.

He rolled towards the passage entrance, and another bullet exploded against the ground where he had been laying. Scott gained the passage and scrambled to his feet, hugging the wall. Another bullet exploded at the edge of the entrance and rock splinters ricocheted dangerously close to him.

Ejecting the yellow barrel from the pistol, he snapped the red one into place. Deliberately taking aim at the arc lamp, he fired. The lamp disintegrated, plunging the mine chamber into darkness.

"Over here, Gus!" he yelled. *"Run for it!"*

There were shouts and a gun flared again and again in the darkness as someone fired wildly.

Scott saw a dim figure hurtling towards him and flashed his torch briefly to locate his own position. The next moment Gus was in the passage, stumbling against him.

"Keep going!" Scott yelled to make himself heard above the blast of another bullet which struck the rock wall beside the passage entrance.

He thrust the other man ahead of him down the passage.

Scott had gone about twenty yards when the solid rock beneath his feet heaved, flinging him against the wall of the passage with a sickening jar. He fell to his knees, dropping his torch. Groping for it, he switched it on and saw Gus scrabbling on his hands and knees a few yards ahead.

The floor seemed to be rippling under them. Deep down there was a menacing rumbling. Another earth tremor. If the roof collapsed…

"Run, Gus!" he yelled, lurching to his feet. "Run for your life!"

He heard a thunderous crash behind him. A shock wave surged down the passage and struck him like a battering ram, smashing him to the ground again. Dust swept over him, choking him, stinging his eyes.

He twisted and flashed his torch back along the passage. The end was blocked by a jumble of fallen rock. The roof of the mine chamber had collapsed. Morales and his gang would not have stood any more chance than snowballs in a furnace.

As he pushed himself dazedly to his feet, a figure loomed through the dust pall before him. It was Gus.

"I thought I told you to get the blazes out of here," Scott gasped.

"You risk your neck for me and then you expect me to run

out on you?" Gus retorted, taking his arm. "Come on! We'll sink or swim together, old chap."

They stumbled on and presently Parker appeared in the torch light.

"Thank Pete you're orl right, Mister Scott!" he growled. "I sent 'er Ladyship back to the river chamber with the perfessor bloke, seein' it didn't seem too 'ealthy down 'ere."

When they entered the chamber, they saw Lady Penelope and the professor by the foot of the ladder leading to the upper passage.

"Go on!" Scott yelled above the sound of the river.

The professor urged Lady Penelope towards the ladder, but as she grasped it and put her foot on the lowest rung, a voice shouted down the shaft from above.

"Stop there! I have a laser gun."

Scott's throat went dry when he recognised that voice. He had thought they had lost the man who called himself the Hood far back along the jungle trail.

Scott flashed his torch up the shaft. The Hood, dressed in green battledress overalls, was peering down, a laser beam gun pointed at him.

"Don't be a fool!" Scott shouted. "You heard those earth tremors. Another might bring the whole cliff down. You'll be trapped as well as us. The mine chamber has already collapsed."

The Hood chuckled evilly. "So much the worse for you and your companions, Tracy. It will make it more difficult to get your ransom."

"Ransom?" Scott repeated. "What the devil are you talking about?"

"Emeralds, my friend. I want hundreds of them."

"You're crazy! I told you the mine chamber's buried."

"Lady Penelope's manservant has a laser beam. He can cut through the fallen rock until he finds enough emeralds to satisfy me. Hurry, Tracy! As you said, the next tremor might bring the whole cliff down."

Scott told himself grimly that whether they got the emeralds for the Hood or not, it was a thousand to one against their being allowed to leave the mine alive.

Far down in the bowels of the earth there was another ominous rumbling. The floor of the chamber shuddered.

"In case your forebodings are correct, Tracy," the Hood went on with a cold smile, "I shall withdraw to the temple and take the lady as hostage. Unless you bring the emeralds, all of you will die. Kindly climb up to me, Lady Penelope."

She hesitated, looking at Scott.

A thin beam of intense blue-white light stabbed down from the weapon in the Hood's hand and melted a hole in the rock floor between them.

"Climb, Lady Penelope," the Hood snarled, "or the next beam will be directed at your head."

Lady Penelope's face had gone pale, but she smiled bravely at Scott.

"I think I'd better humour the gentleman," she said loudly. "I had quite an expensive hair-do before I left England. I'd hate to have it spoiled."

Then she winked at him and whispered, "Leave it to me. Maybe I can deal with the situation. It's your only chance. When I start to climb, flash your torch in his eyes."

Scott nodded, tight-faced. He hated the thought of her tackling that fiend alone, but there seemed little choice, trapped as they were between the laser gun and the possibility of being entombed by another earth tremor.

"Hurry!" The Hood called from the darkness of the shaft.

Lady Penelope grasped the ladder with one hand and began to climb. Her other hand slid into her pocket.

Scott held the torch beam on her for a moment, and then swung it up to stab through the darkness. He saw the Hood squint against its glare. Then Lady Penelope's hand flashed from her pocket and a tiny object glistened in the torch beam before bursting on the Hood's forehead. With a gasp of alarm, he fell backwards out of sight.

"Gas capsule!" Scott shouted. "Good for you, Penny! Let me get at him!"

Suddenly the solid bronze seemed to writhe in his hands like a live thing. There was a violent shuddering and rock debris showered down on him from the shaft. A piece struck him on the temple and he fell to the floor of the chamber, half-stunned.

He was dimly aware of hands dragging him clear and then, a long way off it seemed, there was a roar like thunder and he knew no more.

Scott opened his eyes to find himself sitting on the floor of the chamber, with Lady Penelope bathing a cut on his temple in the light of a torch held by Parker.

Recollection came flooding back and he asked, "What happened?"

Parker swung the torch to the far side of the chamber. It was just a vast heap of rock rubble, reaching up to the roof where the shaft entrance had been. His heart sank. The entrance had been their last line of escape. Now it was sealed.

He saw his own fear mirrored in Lady Penelope's eyes.

"Guess it all depends on Virgil and the others now," he said quietly. "If we can contact them—"

"There's not a hope, Scott," she said. "You must have lost your radio when you fell. It is buried somewhere under the rocks."

"Then we'll have to try burning our way out with the laser beam," he said, struggling to his feet. "Maybe it's a thousand to one chance, but if there are no more tremors to bring the roof down on us, we might be able to get through to the passage leading out to the temple."

"If the perishin' thing ain't squashed flat by that tremor," Parker said gloomily.

"We'll cross *that* bridge if we come to it, Parker," Lady Penelope said reprovingly. "I think the sooner we set to work—"

A shout from the gloom interrupted her and the professor and Gus came into view.

"The river," gasped the professor. "It's rising fast. Already it is lapping over its bank onto the floor of the chamber."

Scott went to the river. Not only was it higher than when he had first seen it, but it seemed to be running more swiftly now.

Despair gnawed at him. If it rose faster than they could cut through the rock fall they would be drowned. Then a wild hope surged through him, banishing despair.

How long had it taken them to reach this chamber which threatened to be their tomb? Five minutes? It couldn't have been much more. The river was flowing much faster than they had walked. If his hunch was right and it *did* flow out into the chasm…

He looked at the others, who were watching him anxiously.

"Maybe we've got better than a thousand to one chance if we're prepared to trust ourselves to the river," he said. "If our luck holds, I reckon we might see daylight in two or three minutes."

For a moment they were silent, staring at the river and the dark low tunnel into which it rushed. Then Professor de Sabata said quietly, "I am not much of a swimmer, my friends, but I think I would rather take my chance in the river than remain here and watch death creeping up on me."

"That goes for me too, Scott," Lady Penelope said.

"Count me in," her cousin said, smiling at her.

Scott looked at Parker, who grinned brashly.

"Seein' as 'ow I promised to give 'er Ladyship a month's notice before leaving 'er service, Mister Scott, I ain't got no choice but to stick with 'er."

"Okay," Scott said. "Then let's get cracking. Leave the laser gun, Parker. It will only slow you down."

"I'm not a bad swimmer," Gus declared. "I'll take care of the professor."

"Thanks."

Scott took the torch from Parker and lowered himself into the water. Holding the torch above his head, he felt firm rock under his feet. The water rose to his waist. In mid-stream it was up to his chest. The swift current tugged urgently at him and he had difficulty in keeping his footing.

He glanced back. Lady Penelope and Parker were already in the water. Gus was following with the professor.

He signalled to them and plunged forward. A moment later the dark maw of the tunnel swallowed him up.

Letting the current take him, Scott concentrated on keeping his head and the torch above water. Fortunately, the river was free of boulders. After he had gone a hundred feet or so he saw, to his dismay, that the tunnel was narrowing and the roof was lowering. Presently he saw that the roof came right down to the water.

But this had been one of the hazards they'd had to risk when they took this desperate gamble.

He filled his lungs with air and dived.

It seemed that he was submerged for an eternity. His ears began to sing, and a red mist seemed to be closing down on his mind. His head grazed the rock roof and he forced himself under again.

Then, when he felt his lungs could stand the strain no longer. Scott broke the surface and saw the blessed gleam of daylight ahead.

Gulping air into his tortured lungs, Scott let the current carry him through the low exit of the tunnel. All at once he found himself in the open air, with sunlight streaming down on him between the towering walls of a chasm.

Some yards away was a gravel beach. Scott swam towards it,

and waded out. Lady Penelope and Parker soon joined him and a few moments later they were all helping Gus and the near-exhausted professor ashore.

Parker took careful stock of their surroundings, surveying the high sheer rock walls moodily.

"Looks like we're out of the perishin' frying pan into the blinkin' fire," he growled. "Take a flippin' fly to climb them walls and if that roarin' noise is what I think it is there's flamin' rapids waitin' for us down-river."

Scott chuckled. "Quit worrying, Parker. You're forgetting International Rescue. That's the roar of jets you can hear, not rapids. I guess Virgil's looking for us already."

A few minutes later Thunderbird Two swept over the chasm.

The great machine hovered over the chasm while they were winched out one by one. Scott was last to leave and as he rose above the rim of the wall he looked towards the ancient temple of the Goddess of Creation. It was half-buried beneath huge slabs of rock and debris that had broken away from the face of the cliff.

"Guess it'll be a long long time before anyone finds that emerald mine again - if they ever do," he mused.

Virgil grinned as he entered the crowded control cabin.

"Lady Penelope's been putting me wise to what happened down there," he said. "Didn't I say you wanted to hog all the fun?"

Scott grimaced. "Brother, if that's your idea of fun, you can have it. Just get me back to Thunderbird One. I need a quiet little fifteen-thousand-mile-an-hour trip to soothe my shattered nerves."

Twenty minutes later, after they had taken the Rolls-Royce into Brains' workshop pod, Scott blasted off on his under jets from the jungle valley.

Scott flicked the intercom switch and his father's craggy face appeared on the monitor screen before him.

"Base from Thunderbird One. Mission accomplished, Dad. Be with you in time for breakfast. Don't forget to tell Kyrano - *six* sausages!"

"Okay, son," Jeff chuckled. "You deserve them. You did a swell job. Virgil tells me you may have disposed of that scoundrel Hood into the bargain."

Scott frowned. "Well, there's an awful lot of rock piled up where we last saw him, Dad, but I wouldn't like to take a bet it's the last we've seen of him. That guy seems indestructible."

Back on the plateau where the half-buried temple of the Goddess of Creation stood, the Hood cut through the last slab of rock with his laser beam and emerged into the open air, sweating and dirt-grimed.

The first thing he set eyes on was his heli-jet, crushed under a huge boulder that the earthquake had flung from the cliff face.

His face twisted into a savage snarl.

"Bah! International Rescue shall pay for this. We shall see who has the last laugh!"

THE END